The Dog Men

The wagonmaster believed Indians were in pursuit of the train but Henry Churl, the official from the Indian Office in Washington, was sure that all the white man had to do was show evidence of good intentions and peace would follow. Army scout Jim Redpath knew better and the kidnapping of Churl's daughter soon proved Jim right.

Now the scout had trouble on his hands and, with guns being issued to the Indians, open warfare became inevitable. The Dog Men were determined to seize ammunition for their guns whatever the cost.

Could Jim halt the bloodshed? Would the cavalry win through? It was touch-and-go.

The Dog Men

John Battle

A Black Horse Western

ROBERT HALE · LONDON

© 1952, 2003 Gordon Landsborough
First hardcover edition 2003
Originally published as *The Dog Men*
by Mike M'Cracken

ISBN 0 7090 7309 7

Robert Hale Limited
Clerkenwell House
Clerkenwell Green
London EC1R 0HT

Typeset by
Derek Doyle & Associates, Liverpool.
Printed and bound in Great Britain by
Antony Rowe Limited, Wiltshire

CHAPTER ONE

THE WAGONMASTER!

Four wagons came dripping out of the water on to the west bank of the Little Powder River. They were the ones drawn by horses.

But the last one got stuck, part-way across, and that was the one pulled by mules, and mules become even less co-operative when there's water up to their bellies.

When they saw it was stuck, a panic seemed to seize the men nearest the covered wagon. Half a dozen were circling round on their horses in the river, and they all began to bellow advice and instructions. On the bank where the four freight wagons were, another knot of horsemen turned their mounts and looked back.

The teamster began to thrash the mules, and his hoarse voice floated far down the rippling water. As he used the whip, he kept looking round the side of the dirt-grey canvas cover, and his manner was anxious, almost frantic. As if any moment he expected to see menace and danger appear on the bank they had so recently left behind them.

A mule started to rear and lash about. Then it got its legs across the traces and was neatly tripped and went under in a flurry of white foam. For a moment there was a danger of another of the mules going under, and then all the horsemen came converging across and somehow manhandled the drowning mule back on to its four legs again.

The riders got wet. They wiped their faces and growled rough curses at the mule. The teamster whipped out again and the mules took the strain and started the wagon to lurching, but still it wouldn't clear the unseen obstruction. Someone screamed inside the wagon. A girl's voice, frightened as the lurching brought things tumbling down upon her.

Then a voice bellowed from the far bank: 'Mick, you get down an' see what's holdin' up them wheels!'

Mick wheeled in the saddle at that. He was big and hulking, unshaven and not too clean. His face was a savage snarl as he looked across at the wagonmaster who had shouted the order. 'Why pick on me?' he grated, but he dismounted, all the same. He knew better than to argue against the man who gave those orders.

He found a long rock across in front of a rear wheel. He was stooping, his head and shoulders completely submerging as he grappled with the obstruction, when someone on the west bank shouted, 'Look out, they're comin'!'

Mick came gasping out of the water, the rock quickly dragged away. Before he could get the water out of his eyes the teamster was standing up on his high platform, his whip lashing madly into the mules. They plunged and got the crazy, lurching wagon into movement and dragged it up the shelving bank.

Mick caught his horse and mounted, beginning to realize that everyone was in a panic and racing towards the other wagons. He looked round.

A lone rider was sitting his horse within the shelter of some scrub oaks that provided fair cover down that long easy slope behind them. There was confusion on the west bank, where the wagons were being pulled round defensively on an open stretch of green. The horsemen were plunging their beasts in behind the cover of the wagons, and dismounting at speed and hurling themselves on to the ground behind the wagon wheels. Their guns were up, muzzles pointing.

All at once everything was done and there was nothing more to do. Then there was silence, the silence of men watching and waiting for momentous things to happen. It was broken by a rich, fruity voice declaring: 'They will be friends. You see if I'm not right. When they know who I am, they will not attack!'

But there was a faint lack of confidence in the tone, and the orator spoke as if the speech was intended to bolster up his own courage. It didn't bolster up anyone else's. The men lay there, silent, not believing what he said.

Together by the squat, ear-ringed wagonmaster were four or five men, including the wet Mick. They were exchanging secret little glances. They didn't speak, but their eyes were puzzled, questioning. The wagonmaster, as dark as any Indian, his face savage and scowling, caught the glances and shook his head. His manner said, 'I don't know what'n heck this means, either.'

That lone rider now rode down to the water's edge. He held both hands wide apart above his head, and came splashing towards them. He came cautiously, because he knew guns were pointing at him, and he knew that men's fingers grew curiously itchy when they were around rifle triggers, and he didn't want to start any lead coming his way.

The tension in the group under the wagons relaxed gradually as they realized that only one man rode towards them, that there weren't more back among the scrub oaks, as they'd imagined.

That Eastern voice that sounded like a mouthful of over-ripe plums, queried, 'Is this an Indian or a white man?'

The wagonmaster shifted, then spat tobacco juice on to an inoffensive ant. He growled back over his shoulder, 'Could be either. We'll find out in a minute.'

This lone horseman was lean and sinewy; he wore a shirt that was of nondescript colour because it had seen too much sun, and buckskin trousers; on his head was a soiled and battered old hat. His face was copper-hued from a life-time facing all weathers, but when he came near enough they saw that his eyes were grey, and they knew then he was no Indian.

Everyone came up from beneath the wagons at that, relaxing gratefully. The lone rider came splashing out of the water. His horse was big as horses went, coal-black and shiny and seeming in superb condition, It was a stallion. There was a Henry rifle in the boot, but the rider didn't carry any other weapon apart from a hunting knife. The men with the wagon train didn't miss a thing. Sometimes a man's life depended on what he saw and what interpretation he put on the things his eyes recorded for him.

The rider sat high above them on his stallion. He looked cool and unperturbed by the angry glances that were shot at him. Men don't like to be found under wagons when there is no real danger.

They heard his voice drawl, 'Howdy, pards. Reckon you acted kinda scared when I showed up.'

The wagonmaster was back among the wagons, shouting hoarsely for the train to get started again. The animals had benefitted by the short rest and at the cries from their team-sters, swinging into their high seats, they began to pull out in line up the long, rutty trail that led through the wooded hill country.

Hearing that wagonmaster's voice above the others, the lone rider's head came jerking up, his eyes seeking the owner. A little glint of puzzlement came to his grey, narrowed eyes. He had the manner of a man who thinks he recognizes a voice, but doubts the value of his own senses in doing so.

Most of the men were getting the wagons round, and they seemed in a hurry, and again they were glancing back to the east bank of the Little Powder River. Two scrub-faced old-timers rode up, one on either side of the newcomer. But they were friendly, he knew.

Then the last wagon – the one drawn by the mules – heaved convulsively and got moving, and for a second the rear curtains parted and the lone rider caught a glimpse of a bonnet within. It wasn't the plain, workaday bonnet he usually saw on this frontier; this was an extravagant thing of frills and ribbons and feminine tucks and what-nots.

He said, 'A woman – or gal?' And his voice was surprised and didn't sound pleased.

One of the old-timers said, 'Sure – women!' And his voice didn't sound any more pleased, either.

The lone rider asked, 'Eastern women?'

'Sure.' The old-timer sighed, as much as to say, 'Any women out here are hell, but Eastern women are too much for any fellar.' He went on, 'There's three – mother, daughter an' a gal travellin' companion.'

Then the other old-timer spoke. He'd been looking closely at the lone horseman. He opined, 'I'd say you gotta name like Redpath, mister. Jim Redpath, huh?'

'Sure.' The hunter looked down on the speaker, with his dark scrubby chin and eyes bleached almost colourless by exposure to the elements. His voice sounded humorous as he said, 'Looks like you figger we've met somewhere sometime.'

'Yeah.' Darky began to roll a cigarette deftly, employing only one hand and only two fingers and a thumb of that one. 'I figger I did once run across you in the Platte country. And I've heard quite a few tales about you too.'

His manner was respectful, as if the tales he had heard about Jim Redpath weren't exactly against the man's character.

Lem, the other old-timer, came in quickly with, 'You goin' to Fort Phil, Jim?' Lem was looking across at his companion. Redpath had a feeling that they shared a secret and weren't happy about it.

Redpath said, 'Sure, that's where I'm aimin'. Reckon you must be goin' there yourselves, followin' this trail.'

They were riding alongside the wagons now, gradually coming up to the front. It wasn't pleasant, riding in the dust behind the last wagon. The mule-drawn prairie schooner was being whipped up to overtake the freight wagons, perhaps at the behest of the lady occupants who wanted to be out of the dust, too.

The Easterner on his placid mount was just in front of them, with a couple of the men. And in front of those was the wagonmaster, with his flat hat and black hair slicking below it and the suspicion of ear-rings to be seen at times. Redpath was urging his mount along as if he wanted to have a look at that wagonmaster.

He spoke to the two old-timers. 'You're in an all-fired hurry, pards.'

Lem spat into the dust. 'We got warnin' there's Injuns on our trail.'

'Injuns?' Redpath was politely incredulous. 'I joined that trail five miles back, an' I never saw any sign of Injuns.'

Lem and Darky exchanged quick glances. Lem said, 'The wagonmaster sure came tearin' in in a hurry a coupla hours back to say there was Injuns back along the trail.'

Redpath's eyes were very narrow now, looking up after the wagonmaster. He was a 'breed, he could tell even from this distance. He had nothing against 'breeds as a whole, but he was inclined from his experience to treat them with caution. Here on the frontier West they were regarded by Indians as well as whites as unreliable, not to say treacherous, in their relations with either people. He was thinking, however, that he had known some fine, courageous men of mixed blood when the Easterner turned and spoke to him.

The Easterner was portly, like a man who liked to live well. He was middle-aged to elderly, and the unaccustomed exposure of the trail had burnt his face fiery red. He sat his horse like a man who wasn't too happy in using four legs where before he'd always been used to two.

He boomed, 'Sir, I couldn't help overhearing your remark. Allow me to say that even if there are Indians behind us, I do not doubt they will treat us as friends, provided we show them we are here on a friendly mission.'

Redpath let his eyes drop, so that the Easterner wouldn't see the doubt in his mind. He knew Indians, and he was not so sure as the Easterner about the innate friendly intentions. He seemed to remember an awful lot of Indians who weren't in the least friendly towards the white man; but perhaps the Easterner knew another kind.

Aloud he said, 'I'm Jim Redpath, a scout and hunter attached to the army. I've bin told to report to Fort Phil Kearney.'

The portly man went on smiling, but in some subtle way his manner had changed. As if he didn't really approve of scouts – or was it hunters?

But he boomed heartily, 'I'm Henry Churl. I've been sent from the Indian Office in Washington to talk peace terms with our Indian brothers. You'll be welcome to travel with us, if you so mind, Mr Redpath.'

Redpath didn't know what his own mind was, for the moment. Like all practical frontiersmen he had no love for the distant, bungling politicos of the Indian Office or for their representatives. Also he preferred to travel quickly, alone, rather than trundle along with a creeping wagon train.

Out of the corner of his eye he looked at the representative of the distant Indian Office. They were all either knaves or fools, in his experience, with a preponderance of the former over the latter. Looking at portly, complacent Henry Churl he decided that this man was more likely to be a fool—

He didn't want to ride on if there was a possibility of the train being attacked by Indians; it was his duty as an army scout to give all the protection he could. He returned to the subject of Indians.

'I never saw no Injuns back along the trail. Mebbe there ain't no need for such hurry,' he said politely.

'I don't think there's any need for hurry, either,' boomed Henry Churl, and perhaps the scout's words gave him confidence, for now he sounded as if he really believed what he said. 'I'm quite sure that when the red man knows my intentions, he will treat me as a very good friend.'

Redpath got the feeling of tension between the two old-timers who still rode on either side of him. They were studiously watching to the front, as if they didn't want to meet his, Redpath's, eye.

Their manner, more than anything, prompted him to ask, 'Why should a redskin want to treat you as a friend?'

He'd met these Easterners from the Indian Office before. They always felt they knew more about the red man than the frontiersmen who had lived alongside them all their lives. Churl would be no exception.

Churl wanted to show off, couldn't resist demonstrating his importance. He was a fool, all right. He repeated, 'I am empowered to negotiate a peace with the Indians.'

Redpath got that feeling again of tension on either side of him, felt suddenly a wave of distaste amounting to hatred emanating from the old-timers. His own voice was brittle hard as he demanded, 'What sort of terms are you gonna offer the Injun?'

He pulled aside. The mule-drawn prairie schooner was lurching up to the front now.

Churl mopped his forehead. 'They are to receive bounties, if they will maintain the peace. They need bounties if they are to live, because the buffalo herds are now so thinned that they cannot support the tribesmen as they formerly did.'

That was a dig at Redpath, because he was a hunter of buffalo for the army.

Redpath ignored the innuendo. He knew there was more behind this peace talk than increased bounties. He asked, softly, 'Anythin' else, Mr Churl?'

He felt the old-timers turn their eyes towards him now, listening for the Easterner's answer. And the Easterner was just not quite so sure of himself and put a defiance into his voice as a cover to this lack of surety.

'Yes. The white man is going to give the plainest evidence of his good intentions to the Indian.' He paused and licked his fat lips, and his eyes avoided the steely-grey ones of the hunter. 'Our troops are to be withdrawn from the Big Horn country, which is to be for all time Indian territory.'

Redpath reined. He sat hunched forward in the saddle.

'The forts – Phil Kearney an' the others – guardin' these roads around the Big Horn? What're you plannin' fer them, mister?'

'Fort Phil Kearney,' said fat Henry Churl deliberately, 'is to be destroyed along with the others, leaving the territory free from our troops.'*

Redpath heard the two old-timers sigh alongside him. It was a long-drawn exhalation of breath that spoke of the weariness of their souls at hearing such rank folly.

Redpath's own voice came out hard and clear. He was no man to finesse with his words. He shocked Henry Churl by his bluntness, so that the portly Easterner almost rocked out of his saddle.

'I've heard fool talk in my time, mister, but what you said just now sure beats anythin' I've ever listened to!' And then it seemed that a cold temper overflowed upon the Easterner from the Indian Office.

'You fools don't know what you're doin'. Destroyin' our forts won't stop warfare – it'll start it! The Injuns can't find food enough in the Big Horn country, an' they'll come out as they've always done, raidin' an' pillagin', burnin' an' destroyin', because they know no better. You, Mister Commissioner, will be responsible for the deaths of hundreds of white settlers, men, women an' kids. Just think of that before you commit yourself to your folly!'

In exasperation he pulled round his horse. He saw a pretty face under that beribboned bonnet, saw anger in those bright blue eyes. Heard the gasp of indignation from the girl leaning out from the back of the prairie schooner—
'What impertinence, to speak to my father like that!'

Redpath politely touched his hat. He saw another girl for a second behind the modishly dressed one, saw an elderly woman fluttering uneasily behind them both. Then he

* Fort Phil Kearney was in fact destroyed upon the orders of the distant bungling politicians in Washington's Indian Office, with the disastrous results prophesied here by Army Scout Jim Redpath

started to ride back down the trail. He wasn't going to keep pace with Churl and his slow wagon train; his temper wouldn't permit it. When he saw folly he spoke out against it.

The old-timers came back with him a few yards. They appeared anxious to dissociate themselves from Churl and his intentions.

Lem spat again and said, gloomily, 'We jes' kinda signed on to act as guards as far as Fort Phil, Jim. We didn't know when we took on.'

Jim nodded. Said, 'Sure, I reckon you old-timers got more sense than to agree with that *hombre*.'

Lem went on, but more softly now, as if afraid of being overheard, 'Jim, I don't like this train. It spells plenty bad trouble, I'm opinin'. I don't like Churl, an' I like his wagon-master a hull lot less, and there's four or five galoots here sticks close to the trail boss an' they all seem thick as thieves.' Deliberately he repeated, 'As thick as thieves!'

Redpath said. 'I never knew an Indian commissioner's wagon that didn't attract the worst rascals in the state.' What he had seen of some of the mountain train guards didn't warm his heart towards them. They had the hangdog look that didn't speak for honesty.

His voice began to shape another question – 'What kinda trouble are you figgerin' on, old-timer?' Then a harsh voice bellowed behind them – the wagonmaster's – and immediately the two old-timers swung their horses round and cantered away.

Redpath rode back to the river, forded across and retraced his steps up the sloping hillside beyond. He went cautiously, rifle ready in his brown, sinewy hands, alert for the slightest suspicion of danger. When he came out on top he had a clear view for several miles back along the trail. There was no war party racing their ponies along the wind-ing, dusty track.

He shrugged. He didn't understand it. The wagonmaster had reported the presence of Indians and had set the train into a panic of a haste. He thought, 'The fellar must have

14

seen a herd o' deer or buffalo crossin' the trail way back an' fancied them into Injuns.'

But it wasn't a satisfactory explanation, not with a man experienced enough to be made wagon boss.

Redpath looked at the sun. Two hours and it would be down. He rode back quickly, so as to join up with the wagon train for the night. They would be relieved to know there were, apparently, no Indians in the district.

He rode at an easy lope until he came to where the wagons were bedded down for the night. The draught animals were being allowed to refresh themselves at a stream that trickled between high banks of vegetation. A mounted guard was along with them.

Redpath dismounted, saw to his horse's comfort, and then walked in between the wagons to where two fires were already brightly burning. A man seemed suddenly to stand up before him in the dusk. Redpath saw his face for a second, clearly illuminated by the glowing brightness of the first of the fires, then the man crossed to one of the wagons.

And Redpath knew him, knew him at once. And his face became a mask of rage; his eyes were snapping with hatred, and almost involuntarily, it seemed, his hands began to bring up the rifle-muzzle and point it after the squat wagon-master.

CHAPTER TWO

WHERE IS ANN?

Redpath sighed and lowered his rifle. That wasn't the thing to do, to shoot a man whose back was turned to you, no matter how much he deserved the treatment. He moved slowly across to the nearest fire. The elderly woman was cooking over it, assisted by one of the young women. Then Redpath saw the girl with the pretty bonnet come hurrying from a wagon with some plates and cups in her hands. Back of her was her father.

They all stared at Redpath as he came into the firelight. Plainly they hadn't expected to see him back after his angry speech with Churl.

Redpath merely said laconically, 'I thought I'd drop in an' tell you. There ain't no Injuns on the trail. You c'n rest in peace tonight, I reckon.'

Churl recovered. He became anxious to show that he was a forgiving man. 'It was good of you to come and tell us, Mr Redpath. Mighty good of you. Won't you join us at supper?'

Redpath would have preferred to eat with the men at the other fire, but politeness made him accept the invitation. In any event, he felt that he ought to give Churl a warning about the man who was wagon boss.

The girl in the bonnet – Churl's daughter, he guessed – was also in a forgiving mood. She was gracious towards the hunter and tried to get him into conversation with her. He suddenly realized that he had become attractive to her, perhaps because of the very virulence with which he had spoken to her respected father. Things like that did happen. But the thought made him uncomfortable. He didn't take much interest in girls. . . .

He saw the other girl, Ann Churl's trail companion. She was bigger than her mistress, though not ungraceful with it. She hadn't Ann's prettiness, but she had a healthy, comely attractiveness that pleased the hunter much more. He found himself watching her as he ate.

Then he came back to the warning he wanted to utter.

Carelessly he said, 'That wagonmaster o' yours – he's called Loup, ain't he? Joe Loup?'

Churl nodded, eating heartily. Redpath thought he heard a movement from the darkness behind him, but he went on, 'You know anythin' about the fellar?'

Churl was surprised. 'Why, no. He offered to be my wagonmaster, and I was pleased to take him on. He got men where before I'd been unable to recruit any. He's a good wagon boss.'

Redpath said deliberately, 'Yeah, he's a good wagonmaster, but I know a hull lot more that don't fit to his credit.'

Joe Loup came sliding out of the shadows at that. He was a head shorter than Redpath, but he had the width across the shoulders and at the thighs. A brutal, stocky little man, with the polished, high cheekbones that betrayed his Shoshone blood. His small brown eyes were glittering and venomous.

'What d'you know about me, mister?' he growled, and his hand was on the gun at his thigh.

Redpath got up, taking his time. Churl and the women came to their feet, sensing trouble. Then Redpath saw other shadows drifting over from the second fire. He faced the 'breed wagonmaster.

'There was a fellar down on the Platte country a few years back who sold guns to the Arapahos – guns he'd stolen from a United States armoury. The Arapahos went on the rampage – wiped out every blamed settler within fifty miles before they got stopped. Three women were killed in that li'l war – three women an' a hull lot o' children. An' men, too.'

Redpath's voice was colder than the Norther that would begin to blow around November.

'That fellar was a guy named – Joe Loup!'

Loup lurched nearer, his face raging and savage. 'They didn't prove nothin' agen me,' he shouted. 'An army captain tried to pin the blame on me, but I got people to show I was a coupla hundred miles away when them rifles was stolen.'

'Sure,' Redpath agreed, his voice ironic. 'You had friends to say the right things about you.' His eyes flickered round the circle of roughnecks who had closed threateningly in on him. 'You got off, but there isn't a fellar down North Platte who thinks anythin' but that you were responsible fer that outrage.'

Loup came raging forward, his men bunching to come in with him. 'You keep your tongue off'n words like that,' he shouted. 'If you don't—'

Then a cracked old voice halted the mounting threat to the hunter. It was Lem's. He was out beyond the firelight, but they caught the gleam of a rifle barrel, and there was another by his – Darky's.

Lem's voice called, 'I reckon you fellars had better mosey back to your own fire. I figger no one's goin' to lay a hand on Jim Redpath while me an' Darky's around.'

That brought them hard back on their heels. They growled, and there was some muttered cursing, but the two old-timers had the drop on them, silhouetted as they were by the fire. Suddenly Loup broke away and strode off to the men's fire, growling unpleasantly, 'OK, let's get back to our food. We'll fix Smart Mister Redpath another day!'

The commissioner seemed to swallow, once the danger was averted. The two old-timers lounged up and, uninvited, came in for some of the Churls' food. Maybe they figgered things wouldn't be too healthy for them across at the wagonmaster's fire.

Mrs Churl, a timid woman, unhappy in her surroundings, served food to them all. No one mentioned the unpleasantness with the wagonmaster. The commissioner got to talking again about Indians. He seemed determined to demonstrate his foolish belief in his own safety in this hostile country.

'I myself have never had any doubts about the redman,' he boomed, warming to his subject. 'Treat him right, and he's as good as the next man.'

Redpath said, 'Sure, sure,' but they didn't know what he meant.

The commissioner kept on talking. 'If I'd had any doubts, Mr Redpath, do you think I would have risked the life of my wife and daughter out here in this wilderness?' He made his voice sound humorous and condescending and Redpath didn't like it.

He wanted to change the conversation, wanted to hear the other girl speak, the companion to Ann Churl.

He said, 'You're kind of risking another gal's life, too, Mr Churl.'

The girl lifted her eyes. They were good, friendly, intelligent eyes, and they smiled at the hunter, and then dropped to her plate.

Redpath, suddenly daring, ignored everyone. Like the plain-spoken man he was, he asked a direct question, 'I sure would like to know your name, miss? Mine's Jim Redpath.'

She flushed, awkward at the attention being unexpectedly concentrated upon herself, but her voice was steady and clear as she answered, 'It's Rewler. Judith Rewler.'

Redpath asked gently, 'What decided you to come so far west, Miss Rewler?'

'I thought it would make a pleasant change from Washington,' Judith said, glancing quickly across at the red-faced commissioner. 'Mr Churl was so sure there was no danger.'

Redpath let his eyes linger on Henry Churl. This man was an outsize in fools, to risk the scalps of these womenfolk in Indian country. The two old-timers were heavily silent, eating and saying nothing, but sharing his opinion, he knew.

The Churls knew what was in his mind, and it made them uncomfortable. Redpath rose and walked over to his horse, not wishing to constrain the conversation with his presence. He rode through the darkness to a hill he had noted earlier, while it was light, and let his horse walk quietly to the brow. What he saw there startled him.

He saw fires – many fires – away in the distance just about where the Little Powder River must lie. His eyes narrowed, straining into the darkness. Fire didn't tell who had applied the light – white man or redskin. But if these were Indians, then it was a mighty great tribe encamped down there.

He watched for a while, then rode back to the wagons. He felt confident that if those were Indians his earlier prophesy would remain unchanged. They weren't likely to attack during the night, because Indians didn't usually like night forays.

As he came in, he saw inside the lamplit wagon of the Churls. They were making their beds for the night. Judith heard him, saw him as he came close within the lamplight. She smiled. It was a nice smile, and Redpath's heart responded to it.

Then Ann's voice came up sharply, and Judith obediently ducked her head and went on with her work. Evidently Ann didn't intend her companion to have any pleasures denied herself.

Redpath smiled and went in between the wagons. He saw Joe Loup and a group of tough-looking *hombres* squatting on their heels beside the dying fire. They stopped talking when he rode by, and he had a feeling it was because he had been the subject of their conversation.

As he bedded down under a wagon in his solitary blanket, he couldn't help feeling that he was disturbing to Joe Loup – he had a feeling that in some way he was upsetting some plan of the wagonmaster's. A curious feeling.

As he had prophesied, it was an uneventful night. He took a turn on watch in the early hours of the morning, but nothing happened more sinister than a sudden, startling howl from a lone, maurauding wolf.

At first light the camp was astir, Commissioner Churl walking about very hearty and brisk and saying, 'Good-morning' to everybody, even the hunter.

Redpath saw Judith go down to the stream for water and he went across to help her. He didn't think there was any danger to her, though the brush was thick and green only a few yards from the stream, but he just couldn't feel easy about women being there in that country at all.

She smiled nicely when he took hold of the bucket and filled it for her. Her voice was cheerful when she spoke. 'I'm glad we didn't have any visitors in the night, Mr Redpath.'

'Jim,' he said. He hadn't been mistered so much in years as with the commissioner's crowd.

'Then it must be Judith.' He laughed agreement. He felt quite at ease with this tall, pleasant girl, and that was an unusual experience for him.

He filled the bucket and they started back. The girl asked earnestly, 'Jim – who's right, you or Mr Churl?'

Redpath shrugged good-humouredly. 'The Indian Bureau! They're right in everything – the only trouble is, the settlers all over America are just so doggone stubborn they won't admit it!'

'That means you think the Indian Office is wrong in everything?' she flashed. 'Tell me, are the Indians as bad as people make out?'

Redpath sighed. Indians were neither good nor bad, but you couldn't tell that to an Easterner. They were merely fighting to preserve their way of life, while hundreds of thousands of settlers were pouring into the country because they were land-hungry and needed it. Two peoples wanting the same land – it wasn't a new problem.

'Often I figure the white man's the worst,' he retorted. 'We get a lot of scum coming up with the real pioneers.'

'Like Joe Loup? I don't like him.' The girl shuddered.

'Joe Loup's a 'breed, more Injun than white. He's bad,

but maybe there's an excuse for him. But there are white men who do just as he does, who're morally worse.'

'You mean, trade guns to the Indians?' She was quick, that girl.

He nodded. 'Trade a gun to an Injun and he kills a white man with it. And that's bad for the Injun, because then we send an army to wipe him out.'

They walked another few yards, and he had a feeling that the girl was worrying at his side. He looked and saw the frown on her brow, the white teeth biting into her under-lip.

'What's the matter – Judith?' he smiled. 'Got something on your mind?'

'Yes.' She looked at him, and it seemed that she was trying to estimate his worth as a recipient of confidence. 'Jim, I – I don't know whether I should tell you this, but – do you know what we're bringing to Fort Phil Kearney for the Indians?'

Something in her manner arrested him. He halted, his eyes startled, guessing.

'Guns,' she whispered. 'Five hundred breech-loading Henry rifles, and fifty thousand rounds of ammunition – brass cartridges, I'm told, though I don't know what that means.'

Redpath was so shocked that he dropped the water bucket and it spilt over his boots.

He exclaimed, 'You can't be right, Judith! I know it's been done before by commissioners, but I thought they'd learned the folly of givin' guns to Injuns by now!'

But Judith shook her head. 'The Indians say they need guns now to get their winter meat. They complain that the white hunter has decimated their herds of buffalo, and they can no longer live unless they have guns. The Indian Bureau has sanctioned it, and Mr Churl has been given the job of distributing them to the Indians.'

' What do they think they'll get by givin' guns to Injuns?' asked Redpath harshly.

Judith shook her head. 'I don't know . . . I've somehow

22

mistrusted it myself all along. Mr Churl is a fine, impressive talker back east, but out here—'

'Out here he don't rate so large, huh?' Redpath smiled grimly.

She nodded; both turned to refill the bucket.

'Mr Churl says that if the Indian has rifles he will not go hungry, and he is convinced that only hungry Indians make war. You heard what he said yesterday when you joined us?'

'That he's promising to withdraw the army from the Big Horn country? Even promising to demolish the forts to please the Injun!'

' Yes.' As they bent to scoop up the water together she looked at him. 'You really believe that will bring disaster?'

He straightened. 'Judith,' he told her, 'the moment them forts are destroyed every white woman within hundreds of miles of the Big Horn, much less in the Big Horn country, will be killed and scalped – aye, an' worse things done to her. Every white child will die, and the men will die fighting to save 'em. White people live out here only because they have forts to hold back the redskin.'

Judith almost whispered, 'It's terrifying, to think that Mr Churl has power to create such mischief!' For some reason she never thought to doubt Redpath's appraisal of the situation; there was such certainty in the way he spoke, and he looked the man he was – intelligent and experienced – so that she never had doubts about him. It was obvious, though, that for some time, even before meeting Redpath, she had had grave doubts about her employer.

'What can be done to stop it, Jim?'

He shrugged bitterly. This was no new situation. The Indian Bureau had been pursuing the policy of supplying arms 'for hunting purposes' to the Indians for a good many years now, and weren't likely to stop it for even more years. Bureaucracy didn't work like that.

'We can't. Not even the army can stop them,' he told her. 'Commissioner Churl is the approved representative of the United States Government, and is pursuing an agreed if wrong-headed policy. We can't do a thing about it.'

She was listening carefully; she was thinking how well he spoke – she had never expected to find men in these wild parts who could talk so sincerely as well as convincingly.

Then she told him something else. 'Joe Loup knows what we're carrying, Jim.'

They were back up the path again with their bucket.

'What do you mean by that, Judith? Wouldn't he naturally know what load you're carryin'?'

She shook her head. 'Until we left Fort Sully, Mr Churl kept secret from everyone what we were taking to the Indians. He said that if the settlers knew, some in their ignorance might try to prevent the guns from going through to the Indians.'

'Mr Churl wasn't dumb when he opined that,' Redpath said shortly.

'When we entered on the last leg of our journey, he didn't bother to keep the secret any longer. That's when I got to know what we were bringing through. I – I haven't been happy about those guns from the start.'

'But Joe Loup – you were goin' to tell me about him gettin' to know?'

'He seemed to get excited when he was told, and after that I noticed that he and Riarn and Mick Culhedy particularly did a lot of talking together, and once I caught him and Jep Connor opening up a box of rifles. He said they were making sure they weren't going rusty, but I didn't believe him. I had a feeling he wanted to be sure there were really guns aboard, and it wasn't just more of Mr Churl's talk.'

Redpath said drily, 'At times you don't speak too well of your employer!'

She tried not to smile, but it broke through. She was a good-looking girl when she laughed. 'At times lately I haven't thought too well of him. You see, Jim, I've always felt it's a curious way to get peace, to give your enemies rifles.'

Redpath started to laugh, and then a shadow fell between them.

It was Ann Churl. Very fresh and very charming, even though she was dressed in a manner astonishing for those wild parts. She was wearing a three-quarter length black riding skirt, with highly polished boots and a very fashionable riding coat.

'Good-morning, Mr Redpath,' she smiled sweetly.

He said, rather shortly, 'Good-morning, Miss Churl.' He wanted to ask more questions of Judith about Joe Loup and his interest in the rifles; he wanted to know what she was suspecting, if she had any suspicions, that was.

He also just wanted her company, preferring it to the brittle charm of the spoilt girl from Washington.

But Miss Churl wasn't to be put off. 'Judith, do go and help mother with the breakfast. I want to do some riding before we start up that awful trail again.'

Judith took the bucket, eyes downcast in the presence of her pert young mistress, and started off for the camp. Redpath called, 'When you want some more water, Judith, just let me know. I'll sure be glad to get it for you.' And that made Miss Churl very annoyed.

She hadn't missed that she was Miss Churl still, while her companion was established on more familiar terms.

But she was in a persevering mood this morning. 'I'm going riding immediately after breakfast, Mr Redpath. Would you care to come along with me?' She smiled winningly.

The scout just stared. It was incredible, to hear someone talk about pleasure riding in the middle of that hostile country. Plainly these people hadn't any idea of the danger that lurked in those hills around them. He looked at her fashionable Eastern riding habit, and thought, 'She'd have to ride side-saddle in that skirt. Guess she'd fall off every few yards among the low oaks back there,' and for a moment was almost tempted to take her for a ride – a very short one.

But politely he shook his head. His plans were made for the day. 'Sorry, miss, but I'm ridin' out myself, right after I see the train headin' on its way. And if I can give you any advice, you'll stick right close to the wagons all the time. If you get out of sight among that brush, you're not likely to come back, I can tell you.'

Ann flushed with swift anger. She wasn't used to being turned down at any time, and to be refused by a rough-dressed, slow-spoken Indian scout was particularly upsetting.

So she exclaimed, nastily, 'Thank you, but I don't need any advice from you,' and she walked away with quick hobbly strides, as fast as her tight dress would permit.

Redpath shrugged. He went and had breakfast and then prepared his horse for the day. He told the commissioner he was going back down the trail to make sure of the Indians whose fires he had seen, and at once Henry Churl proceeded to give him messages in case they were any of the tribes he had come so far to meet.

'Tell them of the gifts I bring,' he beamed. 'That will bring them up to Fort Phil Kearney to meet me!'

Redpath swung into his saddle. 'If they're hostile Injuns,' he told him bluntly, 'I'll keep right out of their way. Good-morning, commissioner.'

The pompous, red-faced Indian commissioner always irritated him and he was anxious to get out of his sight as quickly as possible. He wished he had never met up with the train; for then he could have gone riding easily and comfortably along on his own to his destination. Now, however, conscience wouldn't permit him to desert the party so easily. He felt that the commissioner was travelling with wolves, and was unaware of the even more dangerous wolves all around him.

Coming round the girls' wagon, just as it was about to set off, he heard a swift-whispered, 'Jim!'

It was Judith. Ann wasn't to be seen, and the quiet, mouselike Mrs Churl was hard at work cleaning the breakfast things. Judith hung around the end of the wagon, her face clouding as she saw him mounted.

'I heard you tell Mr Churl you were riding back towards the Indians?'

He nodded. 'I've got a hunch, from the way they're travellin', maybe they're not hostiles as the 'breed thought yesterday.' And then he said thoughtfully, 'Maybe the 'breed also knows that but for his own reasons didn't let on.' But he didn't explain that cryptic remark.

Instead he smiled at the girl. 'I'm goin' back to find out, Judith. You keep to the wagons while I'm away and don't stray.'

She smiled. 'Be careful, Jim. Don't run any risks.'

He waved and rode away down the trail.

After he'd gone Joe Loup said something to his companions and they all thought for a while then gave approval to the plan he had put up. Lem and Darky looked on suspiciously, but didn't say anything, simply because there wasn't anything to say.

And then the wagons were ready to roll.

It was then they discovered the absence of the commissioner's daughter, Ann.

CHAPTER THREE

HE WHO NEVER RESTS!

Redpath rode out of the camp tolerably sure that within minutes the tiny wagon train would be on its way. A short way back down the trail he left it and struck a parallel course through the foothills, keeping perhaps a mile to the south of the track. That way he felt he was less likely to run slap bang into an approaching crowd of Indians, while he felt tolerably sure that he would know when he was level or past them.

Though he had a hunch that these were no hostiles who were following along the trail behind the party, he was too wise to play his hunches too far.

He rode with great caution, pausing under cover at the head of each slope and not proceeding until he was convinced that the brush ahead was clear of lurking enemies.

Then, about three miles from camp, he ran across the recent trail of a horse. It was no Indian horse, he could tell by the shoe tracks, and it seemed to be stretched at full gallop, by the way the toe print was dug deep and the soft earth was kicked up where the rear feet leapt out of their stride.

He looked at it, an uneasy suspicion in his mind. The tracks were circling back north, towards the trail again, and that way wasn't healthy for a rider while the identity of the following Indians was in doubt.

Redpath put his horse to a canter to follow those wildly careering marks. Then, fifty yards or so along, he halted again, stopped by sight of further footprints.

This time, though, they were made by moccasined feet. These were Indians – Indians running in pursuit of the galloping horse.

He had a pretty good idea by now who was riding that horse. Ann Churl! He remembered now that he hadn't seen her around the camp as he set out from it, and he remembered, too, that petulant obstinacy with which she had greeted his advice to stay close to the wagon train and not go riding out alone.

Well, maybe now she was beginning to understand what he meant. Maybe by now she was losing some of her father's faith in the virtues of the red man!

He set his horse to a quick trot. He would do his best to help the girl, but he didn't intend to go rushing blindly after her, for that was no way to tackle Indians at any time.

The trail quickly ran on to a long sloping hillside which was rather sparsely covered with those stunted oaks that grew considerably at these heights. They weren't set too close together, but with their low branches they made for dangerous riding. Redpath saw at once that the Indians, even though afoot, would easily catch up with a horse under such circumstances.

Some time later he came upon signs which told him plainly that he was too late – the girl had been captured. To his trained eye the, evidence was all there for him to read. He saw where a bough had been broken and guessed that the girl had run into it and been knocked off her horse. So much for Eastern side-saddle habits, he thought!

Than he saw where moccasined Indians had gathered round her as she struggled to her feet; then the deep marks of one set of moccasins, as if the owner was carrying a heavy weight. They led across to hoof-prints. Another of the braves had captured the horse and brought it back to carry their burden in triumph to their camp.

Redpath scouted around closely for a while until he felt he had read all the sign there was to be seen. There seemed to be only three warriors in the party, and they were probably out hunting for game. By the pattern of their moccasins they were probably some tribe of the Cheyennes, though this was rather west of the usual Cheyenne country.

Mounting once more, he took up the trail. He knew that the Indians couldn't be very far ahead, and with two of their number walking they weren't likely to proceed fast.

Coming out of the stunted oaks suddenly, he saw the wagon trail below him. The valley hereabouts was clear for half a mile until more oaks and a lot of brushwood grew on the north slopes beyond the road.

The trail itself was deserted, but he had a momentary glimpse of movement on the fringe of those bushes to the north of the track. Then the movement was lost in the thick vegetation.

Redpath took a risk on a watcher being left to look back along their trail. He set his horse riding down to the rutty wagon road along which they had passed so recently, then put it along the track east towards the Little Powder River.

Here again he was taking risks; for he was doing precisely what he had planned to avoid by his earlier tactics that morning. He ran the risk, galloping headlong along that trail, of suddenly rounding a bend and seeing Indians ahead of him – and possibly hostile Indians at that.

It came off, however. A half-mile down the trail, where cover grew right up to it, he pulled into the brush and went racing north as hard as the rising, tree-obstructing ground would permit.

About a couple of miles later he sent his horse circling until he came across a stream which made an easy entry into some wooded bluffs that reared a mile or so still further north of him. He reined at that and considered the situation.

It seemed to him possible that the Indians would make for this valley, because east or west of it the country looked very difficult to cover especially with a prisoner on a horse. He took a chance on his reasoning and prepared an ambush. If he had reckoned wrongly then he would spend an hour or so uncomfortably crouching, waiting for an enemy who wouldn't turn up.

And the fair Ann would be taken to some Indian village for torture and killing and scalping.

He looked at the sun, then deliberately rode his mount across the open ground towards the stream, crossed it and went upstream. When he came to a place that looked good for an ambush he still rode on, but within a few minutes came circling back until he was opposite the spot he had chosen.

Here he dismounted and left his horse to stand among some thick-growing aspens He felt confident it wouldn't whinny when the other horses approached, and it was too well trained to stray away without him.

He crawled back through the tall grass until he was in a position to cover the trail he had just made with his Henry rifle. Like those weapons in the wagons his, too, was a breech-loading rifle, a considerable advance on the muzzle-loader he had used until a couple of years ago, but still far short of the Sharps repeater that had made an occasional appearance so far west. With a seven-shot rifle he would have had no trouble with three Indians, but with a single shot it was different. An Indian could fire three arrows by the time a marksman could fire, load and fire again with a Henry single-shot gun.

He lay down and waited patiently, though flying insects rose from the lush vegetation along the water's edge and proceeded to make a meal of his face and neck. It never was comfortable, lurking in ambush among thick grasses.

But he didn't have long to wait. Only about five minutes later, he saw movement down along the trail that he had made. His cunning in riding right across that valley had borne fruit. They had spotted his tracks and had turned to follow them. Now they were coming quickly up towards his place of ambush.

Perhaps their success of the morning had exhilarated them and made them feel too confident; perhaps they thought that the Great Spirit was being kind to them again and this was yet another foolish white maiden riding alone in the wilderness.

They came up rather faster than good hunters should have done. But even so they were not altogether careless.

The two hunters afoot came first, about a hundred yards ahead of their companion. The third brave was riding cautiously behind on Ann's horse; slung across the saddle before him was the girl herself. She didn't seem bound in any way, but she wasn't moving. Redpath decided she had either been knocked unconscious or was realizing the futility of struggling with the brave sitting over her.

All three wore only breech clouts and moccasins and the single eagle feather of the brave. They were young, sinewy and agile. Redpath decided they would be formidable enemies even though they did not possess a firearm between them.

He let the two foremost braves trot by him. They were within ten yards of him but never suspected his presence. As they came into the thicker brush they proceeded more cautiously. Redpath saw them disappear, then he waited impatiently for the horse-borne brave to ride up. He knew he had at the most five minutes before the foremost braves found that the trail was circling back – and guessed the ruse.

But that brave was suddenly filled with caution. Instinctively an Indian warrior seemed to know when a trap had been laid, and this was no exception. Probably he didn't like the look of the close cover through which his companions had disappeared.

The brave stopped and sat his horse for a few seconds, watching the way his companions had gone. Then he gently urged his mount forward, while Redpath tensed ready to spring.

And then he stopped again, still out beyond the cover. And now those other Indians must have been out of sight for at least two minutes, and that meant so much less time for escape.

Redpath wanted the Indian to ride right in among the bushes. Then he would rise suddenly out of the tall grasses and knock the brave off his horse before he could let out a sound, and then sneak off for his own horse and trot away before the other Indians knew what was happening.

But that Indian now sat obstinately, out of reach of him in the open. Redpath sighed. He wished Commissioner Churl was present to advise him what to do!

He lifted his Henry, looked down the long barrel, saw a brown, unsuspecting face at the end of his sights, and squeezed the trigger.

He didn't want to do it because it made a lot of noise and betrayed him to those Indians within the brush. He didn't like to do it because ambushing a man and shooting him while he was unprepared went against the code of honour that frontiersmen cherished – good frontiersmen, that was. But a girl's life was in danger.

There was an explosion, and white smoke drifted back into his face. He ran through it, reaching that startled horse before it could rear and run away, even before a very dead redskin came toppling out of the saddle.

Redpath leapt on to the beast, then urged it forward towards the brush where his own fine horse was waiting. He wasn't going to leave such a prize for any wandering Indian to pick up.

As they crashed into the greenery, he whistled and that brought his well-trained horse dutifully trotting out to meet him. It probably saved their lives, for as they wheeled to race across the open ground where he had first crossed the stream, the other Indians came running out of the bush.

One let fly with an arrow that wasn't far off the mark, but Redpath lifted his empty rifle in a menacing gesture and both halted in the distance.

They crossed the glade at full gallop, but in the trees beyond it was slower going and here Redpath knew that the advantage was with the Indians.

Then Ann began to stir. He held her flat with his left hand, guiding the horse with his knees. It hadn't been well trained and it responded clumsily, and he wished he was on his own mount. However, there was no time to swop just now, not with the burden of the half-conscious girl, so he kept on as well as he could.

He managed to load his Henry, though that wasn't easy with the girl moaning and trying to get up off the horse's back. Then he heard the Indians close behind, turned and fired – and missed because the horse plunged at that critical moment.

The Indians came running up abreast at that like savage greyhounds, easily twisting and turning among the trees, while the horses made heavy work of it. They were shouting angry war-cries, and their tomahawks were raised against the man who had killed one of their companions.

Redpath saw one of them suddenly streak towards him, about to knock him from his horse with that swinging tomahawk. He waited, timed it as well as that frightened, plunging beast would permit. As the Indian made his last leap to come up with him he swung his rifle in a great arc, holding it by the foresight and letting the heavy butt come bearing down.

The Indian was too intent on his charge to be diverted by that swinging rifle – perhaps he thought he could get his own blow in first. But that fast-travelling butt won. It caught him on the neck, between the right shoulder and his head. At the last moment he tried to pull away from the blow and he probably softened the impact a little; all the same it was sufficient to send him flying head over heels, and he didn't rise from the ground for quite half a minute.

Then the other Indian tried to jump on to Redpath's own horse, following a few yards behind. It made Redpath go circling round, ready to beat him off with his gun, and the brave pulled quickly away. Fortunately at that second the hunter found himself on the edge of some open country, and he spurred his mount into quick flight, his own following obediently close behind.

34

An arrow sang past him, and then another actually hit him, but it was spent and didn't penetrate, though he felt the blow on his side. He knew they were safe with that last arrow, for this open country led right down to the trail. He came thundering down to it, glad to see that it was still deserted – at any rate, deserted of enemies. There he halted to attend to the girl.

She was fully conscious now and crying. He sat her upright before him, and that was the first time she realized that she was saved. Her expression of relief through tears was rather comical, but Redpath wasn't in any mood for humour.

Ann clung to him. 'You saved me! Oh, thank goodness you did! Those horrible Indians—'

Redpath said drily: 'Better tell your dad what you think of Injuns. Maybe he won't talk so much about innocent red men after this.'

Deliberately he rubbed it in; the folly of the commissioner might yet cost a lot of lives.

'If I hadn't killed an Injun an' batted another unconscious, they'd have taken you and done appalling things to you. Then they'd have killed you and hung your scalp up inside a tepee. You wouldn't like to think of your pretty hair adorning some warrior's lodge, would you?'

But her reaction astonished him. He realized that her eyes were shining, and there was an expression almost of adoration on her face.

'You did all this for me? Oh, how wonderful of you!' It startled him. And then he realized that she was holding tightly on to him, and it wasn't for fear of falling off. 'Why did you do it?' she whispered.

'Why?' Redpath stared. 'Heck, wouldn't any fellar have done the same to get a gal outa trouble?'

'Yes.' She hung her head suddenly, and he realized that she was blushing, and still he didn't understand it. Then she pressed even closer to him and said, 'He would – if he loved her enough!'

Redpath said, 'O-o-oh!' A long-drawn sigh of sudden

understanding. He put away her arms and dismounted and then helped the girl off. He was trying to think what to say to the girl, and at last decided that the only thing was to speak the truth to her, even if it hurt her a little.

Gruffly his voice came to her, making her jump. 'You c'n ferget them romantic ideas, Miss Churl. I jes' followed like I'd follow any man or woman taken prisoner by them Injuns. But don't start gettin' to think I'm in love with you.' Almost belligerently he shoved his face towards her. 'I ain't – understand?'

She did. There was no mistaking his feelings towards her. She cried: 'Oh!' and stamped her foot, because there was contempt in his voice and she wasn't used to that tone from men.

Redpath said, grimly: 'You c'n "oh" as much as you like. Here's your horse. Get back to them wagons as fast as you can.'

He looked at her fashionable skirt, torn and soiled by her recent adventure. He didn't think she could get into her saddle unaided. She was startled to find herself being swept off her feet and dumped astride her horse, though her skirt wasn't designed for such work.

But terror overcame her feeling of indignity. 'You're not going to leave me?' She panicked.

'Nope, you're gonna leave me.' He turned her horse along the trail. 'Ride hard an' I reckon you'll be with the wagons before anyone c'n do you any harm.'

She began to weep hysterically, but Redpath had wasted enough time that morning and couldn't go on playing nursemaid to the girl. He called, contemptuously, 'You'll be all right.' And then perhaps he made his biggest mistake, considering the type of girl he had to deal with. He slapped the horse on its hindquarter, calling, 'Give my regards to Judith.' After his contempt for her, Ann Churl couldn't forgive him for that.

He watched her ride away down the trail. He knew she'd be safe enough, for all her terrors. Then he mounted and rode east at a quick trot. He wanted to make sure of that camp on the Little Powder River.

An hour later he broke from wooded country at a point where he could view the ford. The camp was here, among the trees; he could see that by the rising smoke. But he couldn't see tents, couldn't see people from that distance.

He took to cover once again and rode in a wide circle so as to come on to the river a couple of miles upstream.

When he was within half a mile of the swift-flowing water he ran into a party of Indians.

They were scouting but also after game, and he saw them before they saw him. About half a dozen were riding their ponies along a buffalo trail leading from the river. Redpath at once pulled back under cover and watched them.

A suspicion was coming into his mind even as he saw them. When they were about eighty yards away the suspicion became certainty. He recognized the way they braided their hair, the way they fringed their buckskin trousers.

He rode out, right hand held high, palm empty and turned towards them. 'How!' he called.

They wheeled, saw him and came on at a quick gallop. But they meant him no harm.

Redpath said, 'You're Pawnee scouts, huh?' And the Indians nodded and grunted and showed signs of friendliness.

'You come from the camp on the river, huh?' They weren't exactly talkative, though they understood what he was saying, and again they nodded.

That was relieving to know that the Indians who had been spotted on the trial were friendly Pawnees, in the employ of Uncle Sam. He turned his horse down the buffalo trail to ride on to the camp. Two of the Pawnees rode back with him, but the others continued their hunt.

On the way in Redpath asked the name of their commanding officer. When they told him, 'He-Who-Never-Rests,' he knew who it was.

He'd met him in the fighting a couple of years back around Fort Laramie. His name was Captain Robert Riddell, a very brave, very energetic officer attached to the

Seventh US Cavalry. Riddell commanded a troop of Pawnee Indian scouts, loyal, brave men, who now rode and fought with the white men, who had so recently been their enemies.

As they came up to the ford, Redpath saw that a considerable army was encamped on the far bank. There were several troops of cavalry, and even more companies of infantry. He thought in all there would be about a thousand men at the ford.

The commanding officer must have been a seasoned Indian fighter and knew the folly of being caught with his force divided on two banks of the river, so the previous evening he had camped on the east bank, reckoning he could not possibly get all his men and wagons across before nightfall. This morning he had sent out his Pawnees to make sure there was no large hostile force in the district before beginning the movement across. A good commander paid no heed to time: hours meant nothing, usually, compared with safety.

The cavalry had, in fact, already crossed, but then they were highly mobile and could quickly regain the east bank if an attack suddenly set up. On the far bank the foot soldiers were bringing up the wagons in preparation for the moment when the order would come for them to cross.

There was a great stir and bustle and noise, as officers shouted orders, whips cracked and beasts reared and plunged as they took the weight of the wagons on their shoulders and brought them lumbering down to the water's edge.

Redpath saw Captain Riddell sitting on his horse on a mound on the west side of the river. Pawnee scouts were coming streaming in from all directions on this side of the river, riding up and presenting their reports. The two Pawnees who had ridden in with Redpath suddenly grunted, and went galloping up to their commanding officer, there to report.

The scout sat back and watched the scene for a few minutes. During this time Captain Riddell must have been satisfied with the reports, for he sent a sergeant of the cavalry riding back through the ford to present a report to his commanding officer. Almost immediately the word to advance was given, and at once the wagons started to roll into the water and come splashing through.

When he saw the leading wagons snaking across the ford, Redpath thought it a good time to introduce himself to his old acquaintance. Riddell recognized him as he rode up. He was a rather small, very alert man, spare as all cavalry officers should be, with a bedraggled fair moustache. He had a very great reputation for bravery all along the frontier and was feared wherever he and his ferocious Pawnee fighters trailed.

'Reddy!' exclaimed Riddell in delight. 'Are you in on this campaign, too?'

The scout nodded as they shook hands warmly. 'I'm to report to Fort Phil Kearney. They said I'd find work to do.'

'You sure will. You don't know what that work is, do you?' Redpath shook his head, interested, but the cavalry officer just smiled and said no more about the army's plans. Evidently they were still secret at this stage.

It intrigued Redpath. He wondered why such an army should be sent so late in the year to the edge of the Big Horn country.

Captain Riddell spurred his mount up the trail, shouting orders to his Pawnees to go skirmishing, for at least five miles ahead and on either flank. He and a small band of Indian scouts kept to the track, keeping half a mile ahead of the column, now crawling out on to the west bank of the Little Powder River.

Redpath wanted to talk to the cavalry officer. There was a lot of worry in his mind.

'About half a day's march ahead of you is a small wagon train,' he told Riddell. 'I've just ridden down from it.' He sighed. 'You know what's in them wagons?'

Riddell shook his head. Redpath delivered his shock abruptly, bluntly. 'Guns. Guns an' ammunition – presents for the heathen redskin! There's said to be a few hundred Henry breech-loaders.'

Riddell pulled rein, staring in astonishment. 'Guns for the Injuns? What's this you're talking about, man?' He couldn't believe his ears. 'Tradin' guns to Injuns is forbidden.'

'Forbidden to traders, sure, but not forbidden to commissioners from the Indian Office!'

Captain Riddell sat and swore energetically. Like all army officers he detested the well-meaning but bungling Indian Office. It was full of peace-loving humanitarians who yet brought about war, and caused disaster to come upon Indian and settler alike.

But this was astonishing news; and when Redpath said he had been told there were five hundred guns in those wagons, Riddell nearly exploded.

He thumped his saddle pommel. 'Five hundred guns – to be given to the Big Horn Injuns at a time like this!' He checked himself and looked quickly at Redpath as if to see if he had given the game away. 'But of course you don't know, you won't understand.'

He twisted in his saddle and looked moodily back at the cavalry, waiting on either side of the trail to give protection to the slow train that came creeping through the water.

'Give five hundred rifles to the Injuns, on top of what they've got, and there's hardly a man of us will be alive at the end of this winter. You don't know the work we've got to do, Reddy,' he ended.

All the same, Redpath began to get an idea.

Riddell called to a messenger and began to scribble out a report. As he wrote he muttered, 'We'll get the colonel to wire a protest to Washington. Maybe Senate will be persuaded to stop this damn' folly!'

Redpath said, 'Maybe.' He had no faith in the Senate. He thought, 'By the time those fat-bellied senators get around to discussin' the matter, them guns'll be in the hands of the Injuns.'

Probably the same idea came to Riddell, for his pencil faltered, then stopped. Then he looked up, a grin on his small, nut-brown face.

'You game to try'n put a stop to this stupidity yourself?' he asked abruptly.

Redpath was interested. He nodded. 'Sure.'

The cavalry officer tore up the note and sent the messenger back to his former station. 'We'll think about that durin' the day,' he said thoughtfully. 'Now, it wouldn't be a bad idea if some Injuns raided that train an' got away with the guns, would it?'

Redpath saw he was looking at the Pawnees, and caught on.

But then Redpath delivered another blow. 'Cap'n, there's Injuns back in them hills. I killed one this mornin' – had to.' But he didn't say why. 'You know who they are?'

And when He-Who-Never-Rests shook his head he said, 'Dog Soldiers!'

CHAPTER FOUR

DOG MEN!

Ii shocked Captain Riddell, that news. Redpath saw the small, brown face gape open in astonishment, then Riddell exclaimed, 'Darn it, Jim, then we sure are in for trouble!'

Of all the Plains Indians, the Dog Soldiers were the most feared and formidable. Originally they had sprung from the Cheyenne tribe, and were an elite corps of superb, savage fighters trained to a discipline rigorous even for Indians.

Latterly some members of the mighty Sioux Nation in the north had joined the Dog Soldiers and made them the stronger in consequence.

Generally Indian tribes were very loosely led; they made raids but rarely fought battles and never conducted sustained campaigns. But the Cheyenne–Sioux Dog Soldiers were strategists and were led by true commanders, who fought like real generals, planning battles as thoroughly as their US army opposites.

Captain Riddell knew what formidable fighters they were, because he had campaigned against them in the recent wars around Fort Laramie, wars in which Jim Redpath had taken part.

Riddell sat round in the saddle. 'What're we gonna do about this, Jim? The hell, we can't let them rifles fall into enemy hands!' He was appalled.

42

Redpath said grimly: 'They ain't gonna fall into Injun hands, cap'n.'

Riddell's head jerked at the tone; his eyes fixed on Redpath with interest. Suddenly he remembered what a resourceful man this big hunter had always been in their campaigns. 'You got an idea comin' to you, Jim?'

'There can be only one thing for us to do,' Redpath told him. 'We've got to take them rifles off'n that train afore they get given to the Indians.'

'Take?' Riddell looked round to see that their conversation wasn't being overheard. 'Hey, what're you sayin', Reddy? Don't forget that I'm an army officer, sworn to protect Government property an' carry out Government orders. Now, if the Government's decided that them rifles should be handed over to the Injuns—'

Redpath interrupted him drily. 'Come off it, cap'n. You know darned well you'd lose your rank rather than see them rifles get given out, Government order or no order.'

Riddell sighed. 'I guess you're right, Jim. What do you want me to do?'

Redpath answered promptly, 'Send me around thirty Pawnees tonight.'

'Why?'

'That wagon train's gonna be attacked by Injuns – the wagons set on fire an' the rifles an' ammunition destroyed.'

'Them Injuns'll be my Pawnees?' Riddell considered the plan.

'They sure will.'

'It's risky.' Riddell was an unorthodox officer and so was prepared to take risks to avert what would amount to a major disaster if the arms were given out as planned. But this scheme was hazardous.

'Can you think of any other way of keeping them guns outa Dog Men's hands?' demanded Redpath bluntly, and at that Riddell could only shake his head. 'OK, then, let me take the risks.'

So it was that after dark that evening, Redpath rode through the night along the trail after the wagons. With him were thirty Pawnee warriors. They rode for a few hours, and then halted as the moon came up, clear and brilliant, so that the Pawnees could disguise themselves with war bonnets and war paint. Knowing they must be coming near to the wagon train, Redpath sent a couple of scouts well ahead.

About half an hour later, in country that was becoming rougher, with steep hills and rocky slopes to negotiate, and trees all about them, they heard someone racing at speed towards them.

They halted, guns coming up, and then a rider came bursting out of the darkness, and they saw it was one of their scouts.

'What's the matter?' demanded Redpath sharply.

The Pawnee began to grunt out a reply. 'Wagon train him ahead. Him all dead. Wagon train him shot up.'

They didn't need any more information than that. Spurring his horse forward, Redpath led them in the race up the trail.

Suddenly, in the bright, silvery moonlight, they saw the scene, along a stretch of trail that ran between thick bushes and overhanging deciduous trees. A line of silent, covered wagons, with not a soul stirring among them.

They rode in cautiously, and at that the other Pawnee scout came riding from the bushes to join them. The mules and horses were dead in their traces, and near to the wagons Redpath saw other bodies.

His first thought was 'Judith!' He rode up to the Indian scout and rapped out an urgent question. 'How many him dead you find?'

The Pawnee had the answers all ready. 'Sebben.'

'Seven.' Hope leapt within him. Perhaps some had got away, including Judith. He asked, 'Him squaw among dead?'

The Pawnee shook his head. Redpath tried not to feel elated, because to be alive and in the hands of savage Indians was sometimes less to be preferred than death itself.

And this did seem to be Indian work, even in that moonlight. By his horse's feet was the stiffened old body of Darky – with an arrow in his throat.

Redpath sent his men searching all around the scene of the attack, while he went clambering into the wagons. They were empty. If they had contained cases of arms, as Judith had told him, then the attackers had got away with them.

After a while his Pawnees came riding back to report to him. It was too dark under the trees to pick up trails, and they hadn't found any survivors or more dead.

Redpath swung on to his horse then and went back along that trail like a raging fury, leaving the Pawnees to guard the looted wagon train. When he reached camp he leapt off outside Riddell's tent and went in and woke him with the news.

Riddell just said, 'Hell, the colonel must be told about this,' and went running over to where the troop commander's tent was. Redpath stayed outside, and listened to the drone of voices under the lamplight canvas. The sky was paling in the east, and he wanted to be back on his way to the wagons again – he wanted to be doing something, and he realized that his unsettledness was due to the uncertainty of the fate of Judith. He was doing a lot of thinking about the girl lately.

Riddell opened the tent flap and called him in. Colonel John Endricks greeted him. 'Reckon I've heard quite a lot about Jim Redpath,' he smiled. He was a tough, red-faced old man, not at all educated in his speech. All his life he had lived on the frontier, so that though he had never met Redpath, he had heard of the scout's reputation as a man of courage.

Captain Riddell then began to speak, and at once Redpath realized that the two officers had been doing a bit of planning.

'Go back to the train, Redpath, an' pick up the trail of the Injuns. Follow 'em, an' get them guns an' ammunition off them. As United States army personnel, it's our duty to restore them guns to the commissioner.'

Redpath stared. Riddell didn't meet his eyes.

The colonel cleared his throat noisily. 'Sure, Redpath, that's what you've gotta do. Git them rifles back, see? I want 'em back even ef someone's stuck them bar'ls into a fire an' made 'em no good.' The colonel wasn't meeting his eye, either, and now Redpath understood.

He saluted. 'Yes, sir, I'll get them rifles back.' He shook his head sorrowfully. 'I hate to see good guns fall into a fire. Does 'em no good at all.'

He was still chuckling as he went careering back along the trail to his Pawnees. If the colonel hadn't told him to burn the rifles if ever he laid hands on them, he was a Dutchman!

It was broad daylight when he came riding once again into the bush-bordered defile in which the attack had been made. Black Antler swung his pony round and galloped out to meet him. He had the story complete now, the signs being as plain as words to his sharp, intelligent eye. And what he said startled and bewildered Redpath.

Black Antler took him round to show him what he was talking about.

'Him ambush,' he said. 'Men lie in bushes, wait for wagons, an' fire when him alongside. Him killum all drivers.' He pointed to the boots of dead men around them. They were big, broadsoled, not the kind a man wore if he had to put his feet in stirrups.

He took Redpath through a fringe of bushes, and showed depressions where the dry grasses hadn't yet sprung back to their full height. 'Men lie here – an' here.' He pointed.

Redpath frowned. He could read sign almost as well as an Indian. 'That's all?'

Black Antler nodded, his brown eyes fixed on the white man. 'Six men him lie in ambush.'

'Six?' Redpath was incredulous. 'You mean to tell me only six men stuck up this strong wagon train?' He couldn't believe it. Joe Loup wasn't a pleasant customer, but he and

46

his men could be expected to fight with ferocity if cornered.

From that moment Redpath couldn't understand this wagon raid. Black Antler showed him across to a narrow, rocky-walled gully. 'White men him come here with two-three squaws.' He pointed to small, narrow-toed footprints, then to some brass cartridges. 'Him fight, but not much. Then him get on horses an' gallop along trail to Fort Phil.'

Redpath checked over the sign and agreed with the Pawnee's reconstruction of the affair. But it simply left him bewildered. This wasn't like any Indian attack he'd ever known. For six Indians to attack and stampede a force containing the better part of a dozen hardy, trail-experienced men was beyond him. And he couldn't understand the little evidence of fighting.

Surely they hadn't holed up in that gully, a dozen men and three girls, and watched a mere six Indians unload those heavy cases and, take them away?

Yet that seemed what had happened.

Then Black Antler took him to a clearing behind the bushes. It was about fifty yards in diameter, and well-trampled on. Black Antler went to where a trail led out from the clearing and pointed, 'Him six men ride away with packhorses. Him lie in ambush with twelve-fourteen horses waitin' here for wagon goods.'

Redpath's eyes narrowed, staring. He was sure that Black Antler was right, but if so there could be but one inference following upon this evidence – the Indians must have had pre-knowledge of the coming of the wagon train and of its contents.

That alone could explain the ambush, and the packhorses all ready to take away the guns and ammunition. There was a grim mystery about this raid that was baffling – there was nothing that added up right.

One thing, though, he was relieved to find that Judith and other survivors had apparently got away to the safety of Fort Phil. Now he could set about the trailing of the raiders with an easier mind.

He took one look at the glade again, and somehow it became pictured in his mind. He didn't know why, but this scene in some curious way puzzled him. Then he rode back to the wagons. He found a Colt revolver under a seat and stuck it inside his shirt. Normally he didn't like to carry a heavy revolver, because it chafed his side, but he had a feeling that a six-shooter might come in useful for him in this hostile country soon.

Leaving the rest of the Pawnees to wait at the wagons for the troops to move up, Redpath rode off on the trail of the raiders with a dozen Indian scouts.

The trail was easy to follow, for the packhorses were heavily laden and sank fetlock deep into the softer parts of the hillside. Redpath knew that in spite of the lead that the attackers had, he and his Pawnees would rapidly gain upon them.

Even so, the hours drifted by, as relentlessly they followed up hill and down dale, never pausing an instant for rest. Redpath got to looking at the hoofprints so much that after a time he found he couldn't lift his eyes from them.

And after a while his brain began to say, as of that glade back along the trailside, 'There's somethin' about them hoof-marks that don't add up!'

It was baffling, to feel that a solution to some of the mysteries of the past twenty-four hours might be staring him in the face and he not able to see it.

Then it came, suddenly, like a shaft of light on his intelligence.

Suddenly he was balancing his rifle in his hand and calculating.

There were six rifles to an armoury case, and each case weighed sixty pounds gross. OK, then there'd be over eighty cases of rifles alone on the commissioner's train, apart from boxes containing fifty thousand rounds of ammunition. The total weight of the arms and ammunition would be approaching three tons.

He thought, elated, 'That's the explanation of these hyar deep footprints – and that well-trodden glade back alongside the trail.'

Packhorses couldn't carry more than around two hundred pounds apiece on a hilly trail such as this. Then a dozen horses wouldn't even get away with half of the loot.

The conclusion was startling – only part of the loot was being carried away with these raiders; the rest must have been hidden near to the scene of the attack. Redpath thought, 'I figgered that glade had been too well trod over. I reckon the arms are cached there.' Afterwards the horses would have been walked all over the place to disguise the signs of digging.

As he pressed on, in the midst of his braves, he thought grimly, 'Mebbe we'll fix an ambush fer these fellars when they come back to get the rest o' the arms.' Meantime, of course, the thing to do was to try to catch them with the first load in their possession.

Time passed. Redpath rode with his mind ticking over. He'd had a vague hunch at the back of his mind right from the moment he'd seen that raid, and he wasn't the kind of man to ignore hunches.

Now more concretely he was beginning to say to himself, 'That raid was planned. It was organized like no raid I've ever seen.' Packhorses all ready, maybe a hole dug to receive the arms cases.

He voiced his suspicions to Black Antler, riding at his side. 'Black Antler, him raid no made by Injun.'

Black Antler inclined his head. 'Mebbe. Black Antler think Injun would try to get Paleface scalp.' He shrugged. The attackers appeared to have left the little band of white people with easy means of escape along the trail, and that didn't sound like Indian tactics.

So Redpath ran into an ambush just as he was thinking that this was renegades' work, and for some reason he was trying to relate it to Joe Loup, who was treachery personified. Anyway, he was sure it wasn't Indian tactics.

Running Bear, out in the lead, was suddenly seen to reel in the saddle. Instantly a cry went up from the cover of green bushes – 'Hookahey!'

They had crossed the trail of some hunting Dog Men.

CHAPTER FIVE

THE BONNET

There was a mad confusion of brown bodies leaping up from cover, of horses crashing into the open from behind the bushes. Running Bear got back among them, reeling. They saw him snap off an arrow and pull the stump out of his body. Redpath shouted to him to start back along the trail, then began to shoot.

For a few seconds it seemed all over with the little party. The Dog Men were in force, and savagely determined to wipe out the white man and his Indian allies, and they came flooding along the trail towards them.

Redpath yelled for his men to turn and run for it. They would have to abandon the trail now and try desperately to save their lives.

The hunter stuck his Henry away. There was no time for reloading. He pulled out the revolver, as the Indians came screaming in to the attack, and opened up at them. That six-shooter really saved them, for at such range it was deadly, and even the Dog Men wilted before the fire.

They pulled away, getting in the path of the following warriors, so that there was an unholy mix-up on the trail made by the packhorses, and that gave Redpath time to wheel his mount and go racing after his men.

It gave them a precarious start, and they made the most of it. Lying over the necks of their horses, Pawnees and white man alike went at their maddest pace down the wooded hillside. Behind them, recovering from the tangle, leapt the Dog Men, screaming again the dreaded war-cry of their kind – 'Hookahey!'

Redpath rode as straight as he could for the Powder River, knowing that if they could swim across ahead of the Dog Men they could hold the warriors at bay until the darkness of approaching night. Then they would be safe, even outnumbered as they were.

But the broad, swift-flowing Powder River was a good distance off, and the Indians' ponies were fresher and began to gain on them.

The war-whooping Dog Warriors were right on their heels when they leapt a small, rocky-bordered tributary, and Redpath made a stand for it. They wheeled unexpectedly across the little barrier and emptied their guns into the yelling horde.

It sent them reeling away, falling back on to the main body of the Dog Men, who were coming up behind. For several minutes they fought a battle across the little stream, hurting the Indians, and taking a few wounds themselves from flying arrows. It gave their horses a chance to recover a little wind, and that was vital just then.

Suddenly Redpath gave the order to race away again. They jumped their mounts into the bushes and streaked off. The Dog Men thought it was a trap and came over the stream with some caution, and that gave Redpath and his Pawnees chance to get a lead again.

Now they flogged their horses into the best speed they could make, for ahead of them was the willow-lined fringe that marked the great Powder River. They had a mile to go, and the savage Dog Men were gaining on them all the way. Redpath rode behind his men, loading his revolver and firing back over his shoulder, but at that pace his aim wasn't good.

They were just ahead, though, when finally their foundering horses ran into the cool waters of the Powder River, and that was all that counted. The shock of the immersion seemed to revive the beasts and they began to swim out for the western bank as a shower of arrows came spinning out after them.

They were saved by the fast-running current, which hurled them away from the warriors on the bank.

A few Dog Men rode in and set their mounts to swimming after them, but most of the Dog Soldiers raced parallel down the river bank, shouting their war-cries and taunting the Pawnees for being runaways.

In time the weary band made the far shore. Those Dog Soldiers swimming after them had turned back to their comrades long before this, knowing that if they were caught in midstream when the white man or his Pawnees got to their rifles, they would never survive the crossing. Even a blood-lusting Dog Soldier gets sense into his skull at times, thought Redpath grimly, watching them retire.

The range was too far for effective fire, so Redpath ordered his vengeful Pawnees to keep their weapons silent. They lay about, resting themselves and their mounts. They were waiting for nightfall, so that their departure would be unobserved by the distant, watchful Dog Soldiers. And Redpath had no intention of departing from the river bank while there was daylight, because he didn't intend to give the Indians a chance to cross and set up pursuit again before dark.

Night came. Just before darkness the Dog Soldiers gave in. They stood in a gesticulating bunch across the river from them, shouting contempt and rude remarks, then turned and rode back inland.

Redpath sighed with relief. Dog Soldiers in force weren't to be despised. They had been lucky in getting away from them so lightly.

They mounted when they were sure that the Dog Warriors had gone, and rode first inland out of sight of the river, then northwards, following its winding course. After half an hour, when it was too dark for further progress, they halted and camped down for the night.

It was cold, but they slept without the warmth of a fire.

For this was truly enemy country, and there was no knowing what Indians might be across this side of the water.

When it was barely light next morning, they rose stiffly from their blankets, ate hard tack washed down with spring water, then mounted and rode north and eastwards until they came again to the Powder River. Half a day later they came to the group of settlements known as Sweet Water.

Here the land was open and the soil rich, and it had encouraged some brave pioneers to settle and farm the country. For protection against the Indians, the settlers had built their cabins fairly close to each other, so that from a distance it gave the appearance of a scattered village along the edge of the river-bank.

In all there seemed to be about forty or fifty cabins, most of them almost as primitive as an Indian wickiup, but a few were sturdily built of interlocking logs so that they resembled fortresses in miniature.

As they rode in they saw that the community was gifted with a store that sold everything from ploughs to pins and pans, and was in addition the local saloon besides.

Riding in among the scattered homesteads, Redpath and his Pawnee followers attracted a lot of interest. Little of it was friendly, for the settlers could never make up their minds which was the bigger evil, the Indian Bureau in Washington or the War Department in that same city.

The Indian Office insisted that the savage redskin could be won to peace by sweet words and huge annual payments of good American dollars which the white man had to find out of taxation. While the army bluntly held to the opinion that the only good Indian was a dead 'un.

In pursuance of this latter belief, when the army struck they struck hard, and battles often became massacres. The inevitable result was that the sore and chastened Indian survivors promptly rode off and took it out of isolated settlers, adding massacre to massacre.

When they saw Indians riding into the settlement they reached for their guns, and when they realized that these were US army scouts they put them down tardily, reluctantly. For to these settlers an Indian was an Indian irrespective of which side he was fighting for.

To avoid any possibility of trouble with touchy settlers, Redpath ordered his men to keep along the river-bank, thus avoiding most of the houses. He instructed them to look for signs of the passage of those laden horses that they had been following the previous day, though he didn't think they would have much luck.

There was a ferry that operated across the Powder River at Sweet Water – a big one, capable of taking half a dozen horses and riders at a time. Redpath guessed that if the renegade raiders were heading for Sweet Water, then they would use the ferry in preference to fording across at some more distant point. He thought, 'If they came in late last night they could have smuggled those arms into Sweet Water without any of the settlers here knowing anything about it.'

Though why he should think the destination for those arms could be this settlement he didn't know. It was speculation, based upon the knowledge that the route of the raiders had been roughly pointed towards this section of the Powder River. Also, if white renegades were in the party they would for certain have as their base some remote settlement such as this. . . .

The ferry was downstream a few hundred yards, so Redpath first rode over to the store, dismounted and walked in. It was a dull, windowless place, lighted only by the sunshine that reflected in through the doorway. There was little order in it, with sacks and bales, boxes and oil containers stacked irregularly against the solid log walls. The centre was cleared, however, and here there was a long, not over-clean plank table around which people gathered when they wanted a drink.

Redpath never drank, so he didn't join the inevitable few already knocking back a bottle of rot-gut at that time of the day. They looked just ordinary settlers, rough but all right, probably in for supplies and exchanging news before riding off to their primitive, comfortless homes again.

One of the men, however, rose from the table. He was a big, hairy-armed man, gone fat with too little work around the place. A surly, suspicious individual, though probably decent enough once he got to know you, Redpath summed him up. He appeared to be the storekeeper.

Redpath exchanged greetings. The storekeeper evidently hadn't heard about the arrival of the Pawnees and thus Redpath's connection with the army, but that didn't make him any more friendly.

The hunter took a seat on some sacks of grain. He told the storekeeper straight out what he was after.

'I'm following some men who robbed a train of wagons goin' through to Fort Phil. There's maybe a dozen or so in the party, probably six of 'em bein' Injuns or 'breeds. But I think most are probably white men.'

'Stickin' up a wagon train, huh? That's renegade work.' The storekeeper was getting a bit interested. The other men were listening, too.

'Sure, renegade work. They attacked it to get possession of some ammunition and guns that were being taken to Fort Phil. My guess is they're goin' to trade them guns to Injuns.'

He was watching the storekeeper narrowly as he spoke, ready to spot any guilt if it showed. After all, a storekeeper was a man who often did trade with friendly Indians, and most weren't very scrupulous in their dealings.

The storekeeper knew what was behind that keen glance, and he snarled unpleasantly. 'The hell, the only part of a gun I'd give an Injun is a bullet. I know nothin' about them guns. I ain't seen no men come ridin' in here with packhorses.'

That made Redpath sit up and take notice. He racked his brain but couldn't remember ever mentioning packhorses. It might be that this sullen-faced man knew something, after all, though on the other hand it was logical almost to suppose that raiders of an arms train would need pack-horses to carry away their weighty loot.

'Who are you, stranger?' demanded the storekeeper unpleasantly.

Redpath shrugged. 'I'm a scout attached to the US army.'

The men looked at each other. Then some of them sighed as if to say, 'More trouble!' It was plain that these settlers didn't welcome the presence of soldiers close to their holdings.

The storekeeper said nastily, 'Goldarn it, if you army people would only keep right out of our way we'd get along fine! We don't do badly with the Injuns locally at all, not since we gave 'em food during the bad winter three years ago. Don't you start an' sour 'em up agen us now!'

Redpath rose. There was evidently no helpful informa-tion coming from these men in the store, so he decided to move. He said drily, 'Maybe your Injuns is friendly, but I'll give you a tip. Maybe you'll be glad to have a United States army in the district one fine day!'

One of the men spat and said, 'Never!' But Redpath was watching something out in that sunshine beyond the door-way as if fascinated – as if his life depended on it almost.

'Why should we be glad of soldiers?' the same man continued when the hunter didn't speak.

Redpath hardly heard him. He was walking slowly towards the doorway.

'I said why?' snapped the man. He was touchy, and didn't like to feel slighted.

That brought Redpath back to the present. Brought him back from a river and a ford many miles away – from that first time he had seen pretty Ann Churl.

He said, rather hurriedly, 'Because there's a band – maybe the whole tribe of Dog Warriors hunting just across the river. Better stick close to your scalps, brothers, if you don't want to lose 'em to those fiends!'

A girl had tarried in the doorway, inspecting some metal-ware. Now she was walking towards the river.

And that girl was wearing a bonnet which Redpath felt sure was the one he had first seen adorning the fair curls of the commissioner's spoilt daughter.

CHAPTER SIX

ARRESTED!

Redpath could say for certain the identity of one horse, once seen, against another. Likewise he could tell at a glance the tribe to which an Indian belonged, though there were not many white men who could make that same boast.

But when he came to bonnets he was on foreign ground. He was ready to swear that this was the same bonnet that Ann Churl had worn, but inexperience in such matters put the brake of caution on his words when finally he caught up with the girl. Vaguely in the back of his mind was the thought that perhaps such bonnets were easily copied, and therefore there might be lots of them all over the American continent, only he just hadn't noticed them before.

So when the girl was about to turn in at a gate where a vegetable patch fronted a crude wickiup by the river his manner was reserved.

'Ma'am, your pardon,' he said politely, removing his hat.

She halted and turned, one hand on the gate. She was about seventeen, though a fully developed woman at that age. She was pretty, though it was the flashy brilliance which spoke of mixed blood. Her dress was poor and dirty and her feet were bare underneath it. In distinct contrast was that gay, be-ribboned hat on her dark, greasy tresses.

She smiled very quickly when she saw the hunter and did

a lot of welcoming with her eyes, but he was not there for play and ignored the invitation.

'That's a nice hat you're wearing,' he said slowly.

'You like it, huh?' she said archly, preening underneath it.

'Sure I like it. Maybe you'd tell me where I could get a hat like it,' he said cunningly.

She asked, 'You got a girl?' She didn't seem to like the thought.

'If I had a bonnet as pretty as that, maybe I could get me a girl.' he countered.

She giggled. 'If you was a smart guy, maybe you could get a-holt of a bonnet like this without much trouble.'

Redpath felt he was getting somewhere. 'You tell me, if I was a smart guy where would I look for one?' he asked.

And then a man was standing between them. He must have come quietly around the paling fence from a long, low hut that was built on the riverside. He was plainly the girl's father, though there was no coloured blood in this man. He was short, stocky, with a growth between his small brown eyes that gave him a curious appearance. Redpath had a feeling as if the man was lurking behind himself.

He was a suspicious man, ready to retire and run away. Just now, though, he seemed uneasy and apprehensive. He said quickly. 'What're you talkin' about, Marie? Don't you know not to talk to strange fellars?'

Marie said, pouting. 'I wasn't doin' no harm. He was just talkin' about my new bonnet—'

Her father grasped her by the arm. He was looking all the time at Redpath, but he was pulling on the girl, tugging her arm urgently, trying to get her indoors while he spoke: 'This ain't no new bonnet, mister. Honest, it ain't. She's had it years.'

'Why—' Marie's gasp of astonishment changed to a yelp of pain as sharp fingernails dug into her tender flesh.

'Shut up, you!' snapped her father. 'You get inside an' don't talk to no more strangers, do you hear?' Marie was pushed into the wickiup and then the man called down to the gate, 'I don't speak to no strangers, either, so you'd best be goin', mister.'

Then he went in and closed the door, though it was really too hot to be inside a wickiup without the door being left open at that time of day.

Redpath went back for his horse, then rode after his Pawnees. He had little doubt in his mind now that he had stumbled, if luckily, upon the trail of the train robbers here in Sweet Water. That hat could only be the one that Ann had worn; the obvious lies from Marie's father merely removed any lingering doubts from his mind.

It meant that if Ann had got away safely with her father – and he felt that the reconstruction of events as detailed by Black Antler would be correct – then probably some member of the stick-up gang had lifted the bonnet during the looting of the train and presented it to his girl friend when they returned to their hide-out in or near Sweet Water.

The Pawnee scout leader reported no sign of the men they were after for the next three miles up the bank. No one had tried to make a crossing, though the river was shallow enough to ford at one place, he told the hunter.

Redpath nodded, accepting the report. He didn't think it likely that with a convenient ferry to hand they would attempt a hazardous crossing of a ford with their heavily burdened horses.

So he went back to where the big flat pontoon was tied to a stake on the edge of a gravel bend. As he got nearer he began to realize that the boat must be pretty close to the wickiup in which Marie and her father lived, and then he saw that that long hut that was neighbour to the wickiup was probably the boathouse in which the ferry was kept during the wet winter months.

He drew rein. He began to think at that moment that the ferryman would turn out to be a man with a curious lump of flesh between his eyes.

There was an idler, an old man without teeth and beyond the age when he could be expected to work overmuch, who was sitting near to the ferry. Redpath rode over to him.

'Howdy, old-timer,' he said. The old man mumbled in his gums.

'Are you the ferryman?'

The old man found voice. It was cracked and surprisingly high. 'No, sir. I ain't no ferryman. You'll find him back among them wickiups.'

Redpath looked at the wickiup in which Marie had gone. 'He wouldn't be a fellar with a bump between his eyes, huh?'

The old man spat, then said, 'He would. By dingo, you got him first time, stranger. Right a-tween the eyes, I reckon,' and he cackled at his own senile wit.

So Redpath abandoned all thoughts of speaking to the ferryman. He knew it would be a waste of time to question that uneasy little man with the bump between his eyes. That fellow was as much in this as the actual wagon robbers themselves.

He looked around for tell-tale tracks, but there weren't any. The beach on which the pontoon grounded was shingly and incapable of taking footprints, while beyond it was a regular dirt road which split off into well-trodden paths that led to all the dwellings in the Sweet Water settlement.

He rode up a few of them, then abandoned the search. It was useless to try to distinguish one set of hoofprints from another. The paths were just a hopeless confusion of hundreds of footmarks – a whole summer of them.

The hunter rejoined his patiently-waiting Pawnees.

'We'll camp here for the night,' he told them. 'Maybe something'll turn up.'

But nothing did. If the wagon robbers were hiding out in that settlement, then they were doing it very successfully. Redpath knew that most of the settlers would readily turn on renegades who were prepared to sell arms to their enemies, the Indians, and because none came forward with information it indicated a very good hide-out.

In fact, of course, it would be easy for any small band of men and their mounts to hide away in one of the more remote farms around Sweet Water, and Redpath guessed that that was where they would be right now. The worst of it was, by now they must surely know that a search party was in the district and that would make them doubly careful.

All next day he and the Pawnees hung around the place, but he knew it was a waste of time, even as he did so. He began to think the only way to capture the raiders was to return and watch over the buried arms and seize anyone who came along to dig them up. But hanging round Sweet Water wouldn't do any good; the raiders could laugh at them from their hiding-place for just as long as they kicked their heels in the neighbourhood.

The hunter went round to as many homesteads as he could, but no good came as a result of his search. Then, immediately before leaving Sweet Water, he rode up to have a final word with the sullen, towering storekeeper.

He talked plain to him. 'I told you there's a party of rene-gades hidin' out around Sweet Water, who have a lot of rifles an' ammunition with them. I think they're out to do secret trade with Injuns. All right, if you know what's healthy for you, you'll keep your eyes skinned and send word to Fort Phil if you get suspicious on where them crit-ters is likely to be hidin'. Sabe?'

The lumbering, hairy-armed storekeeper seemed to speak with sincerity. 'Ef I find anything, I'll let you have word. Me, I'd shoot any snake that tried to sell a gun to a murderin' redskin!'

Redpath this time came to the conclusion that the fellow was sincere. And judging by the chorus that came from the three or four other men in the store, there were others of like mind in Sweet Water.

He hesitated, then took the storekeeper into his confi-dence. 'I've got an idea the ferryman knows about them raiders.'

The storekeeper looked quickly at his companions. One farmer pursed his stubbly lips and said, 'I wouldn't put anythin' past that fellar. He keeps bad company – that's where he got his 'breed wife.'

Redpath said, 'I guess I couldn't get anythin' out of him if I tried, but you might keep your eye on him for me.'

He didn't tell them that his plan was to send somebody back to keep watch on the neighbourhood – either that or return secretly himself.

It was useless leaving the Pawnees here, because they were too conspicuous – as scouts they were fine, as spies they didn't have a chance. So he was planning on a quick return to Fort Phil in order to try out new plans for getting hold of those vital arms.

It was just over a normal day's ride to Fort Phil Kearney, but they pressed hard in the hope of riding in soon after nightfall. In the middle of the afternoon there was a slight delay, however.

The foremost Pawnees reported movement on the skyline ahead, but after some scouting, a report came back to the waiting party to say it was another party of Pawnee scouts apparently on their way out from Fort Phil.

They rode across the grasslands to meet these other members of their troop. There were five of them. They spoke at length to Black Antler, but Redpath understood most of what they said without need for an interpretation.

He-Who-Never-Rests had turned out all his scouts in order to find what Indian movements there were around Fort Phil Kearney. Apparently they had rested for one night only at the fortress, and then they had been despatched in small parties in all directions from Fort Phil. Yes, He-Who-Never-Rests had also taken the saddle with one of the parties.

The hunter thought, 'That sounds as though they've got wind of considerable Indian movements, back at Fort Phil, for Riddell to go off so quickly without first restin' his men.'

For all his impatience and desire for action, the captain was a good officer and always looked well after his men where possible. For him to send them out immediately following a fortnight's hard work along the trail suggested serious news about their Indian enemy. Redpath wondered if the serious news meant that more than the Dog Soldiers were moving into the neighbourhood. Maybe the Cheyenne tribe and the mighty Sioux Nation were also moving towards the Big Horn.

If so then perhaps Riddell had been right in suspecting a leakage of army planning. Redpath was guessing at the secret behind the army's move to Fort Phil, but if it was what he thought it to be, then he knew that it would bring upon them the full ferocity of all the Indians for many hundreds of miles around.

Redpath said goodbye to the scouting party, but before they moved away Black Antler announced that he wanted to go with them. He didn't want to go to Fort Phil, preferring to remain on the war trails with his brother Pawnees.

At this the other Pawnees chorused a quick request to take the trail also, and as he had no need for them so near to Fort Phil, Redpath let them go. Only Running Bear and the second wounded Pawnee would come along with him, though even they wanted to ride with Black Antler.

They parted, and Redpath rode as hard as the wounded Indians could stand, so that less than an hour after dark they came before Fort Phil.

The fortress stood back from a tributary of the Powder River, on a commanding eminence right among the feet of the Big Horn Mountains. It was the usual stout frontier fort, consisting of a central blockhouse with some smaller buildings around it, set within a high palisade of sharp-pointed logs. The whole was built from stout lumber felled back up the hillside – and in felling it they had left the rear clear of any cover that could protect an attacking enemy. It was well built, and in a good position.

But Redpath saw none of that when he rode up to the big gates in the dark. He remembered every detail quite clearly, however, from two visits to the place on previous campaigns a few years back.

There was a challenge as they splashed up through the water. The hunter shouted, 'I'm Jim Redpath with a couple of wounded Pawnee scouts. Let me in!'

The sentry shouted. 'Who d'you say you are?'

'Redpath. Jim Redpath.'

There was a curious pause after that; the sort of pause that could be made by a man taking time off to relay some interesting information to another.

Then the sentry shouted, 'You c'n come up to the gate now, Redpath. We'll open up fer you.'

The hunter and the weary, wounded Pawnees rode slowly, cautiously, up the rough trail that led to the big swing gates of the palisade. Above it was a sheltered platform on which stood several dark forms, watching to make sure this was no ruse to break into the fortress.

The gate opened for them to enter and they rode in. Just within was light from lamplit windows and from a couple of hurricane lamps that were being brought out of the guardroom, the better to inspect them by.

The guard commander, a sergeant of the 21st Infantry, came up to greet him, and Redpath noticed idly that most of the guard seemed to have turned out, too.

Noticed, suddenly, that all were armed with rifles.

And those rifles were all pointing at him.

The guard commander, an old campaigner with plenty of moustache, said roughly, 'You say you're Jim Redpath?'

The hunter watched those pointing rifles in the yellow light of the swinging hurricane lamps. His eyes were narrowed, trying to work this out and failing.

'I am Jim Redpath. I guess there'll be some men here who c'n vouch for that. One will be Colonel Endricks.'

The sergeant said, 'OK, Redpath, I'll take your word for it. We'll leave the colonel in bed until tomorrow, I guess.'

Redpath said. 'Fine. That's where I'll be as soon as I c'n get my Pawnees doctored an' looked after.'

One of the lamps was being held close to him now. It was being held so that the full radiance fell on him, as if to guard against any hidden movement on his part.

Then the sergeant said, 'I'll look after your Pawnees for you, Redpath. I'm arresting you, accordin' to the orders given in case you turned up, and I reckon you'll sleep tonight in the guard cell.'

Redpath exclaimed, 'What—'

Then something hard was shoved roughly into his back.

'Don't argue. You heard what the sergeant said?' One of the guard was covering him from behind. 'An' stick them hands up, can't you?'

Redpath's hands climbed. He was astonished, but he kept his temper. 'What's bitin' you? Why were you given orders to take me prisoner when I came back?'

The sergeant said brusquely, 'You'll find that out in the mornin', when the fort commander has you before him. Now – march!'

He barked the word so loudly, it made the hunter take a quick step forward. After that the jabbing gun in his back kept him going.

One minute later he was in the guard cell attached to the guard-room. It was a very small, solid room with a small, barred opening for a window, and a door that would have defied a battering-ram for a good while. In fact, it was very much a prison cell, and the stamping of a sentry's feet outside served to emphasize the fact.

He was given no light, but he fumbled around and found a bench on which was one blanket. He hadn't the faintest idea why he was in this predicament – there wasn't so much as one ray of light to tell him. But he wasn't the kind of man to lose sleep even under such circumstances, and within minutes there was no need for the sentry outside the door.

Jim Redpath was sleeping the sleep of a very tired man.

They brought him breakfast next day, but when he questioned his gaoler the fellow just looked queerly at him and didn't say anything. So Redpath ate his breakfast and then waited until they came to take him before the fort commander.

About eight in the morning the sergeant guard-commander came with two soldiers and ordered him to go with them before their superior officer. Redpath fell into step and marched out of the guard cell. Out in the sunshine, they went marching across the open parade ground within the palisade. There were a lot of people about, soldiers, civilians, a few Indians – and a girl.

It was Judith.

He was being marched straight across towards her. At that moment he hated the indignity of his position, but there was nothing now he could do about it. He had to submit to being marched between two armed guards like any wretched felon.

She saw him, and her mouth opened in surprise. He thought for one second that she made an involuntary movement towards him.

Then she hesitated – hesitated and then slowly turned her slim back towards him.

She did not turn as he was marched by, and he did not attempt to call out to her. She didn't want to speak to him.

That was probably the most puzzling part of the whole affair. He certainly had never done anything to warrant such a snub from the girl.

CHAPTER SEVEN

THE SENTENCE

Major James Leabridge was the officer commanding Fort Phil Kearney at that time. He looked up as the hunter was marched into his presence with a great stamping of feet and barking of orders. He was a thickset, middle-aged officer, heavily moustached and grey. In a crisp, military tone he read from a paper:

'James Redpath, you are charged that while in the service of the United States Army as a hunter and a scout you behaved in a manner prejudicial to the good name of those you serve.'

Redpath's eyes jerked open with astonishment.

'You are charged with assaulting a civilian woman, the daughter of an Indian Office representative, namely, Miss Ann Churl.' He threw down the paper and barked, 'Wal, Redpath, what have you got to say about that?'

Redpath just looked at him. For a quarter of a minute he couldn't think of anything to say. Then he exploded, 'What'n the tarnation—' He checked himself. 'Who says I did all that?'

'The charge,' rapped the major, 'was laid by Miss Churl herself.'

'Then,' Redpath said grimly. 'Miss Churl's tellin' lies.'

'Stop that talk!' The major was looking with contempt at him. 'No girl would make up a story like that.'

Redpath said, 'No?' He was thinking, 'This one has.' Then he tried to puzzle out why.

It slowly began to dawn on him. He remembered that saying about hell having no furies like a woman scorned – and he had scorned her silly, romantic advances along the trail. Worse, he had introduced the name of another girl – her own servant – right at that unfortunate time. He'd blundered tactlessly, there.

She'd been pretty hysterical, too, and in a mood of hysteria a girl was capable of any fantastic charges or action.

Wrathfully he exclaimed. 'The hell, major, I saved that gal's life.'

This was a poor return for what he'd done for her. Then he thought, 'She's too shallow; she doesn't understand what I saved her from.' If she had, she could never have made such an accusation against him.

The major spoke shortly. 'Bluntly, Redpath, it's your word against the girl's. She says you met her on the trail and tried to make love to her and handled her roughly. Her father and others with the wagon train testify to her distressed condition when she came riding in. I'm afraid that's all against you.'

The prisoner faced him boldly and demanded: 'You fetch Miss Churl in before me an' see ef she sticks to her story.'

The major rose. 'Miss Churl is in no condition to be distressed again by you, Redpath. I'm sorry, but the evidence is against you. I believe the girl's story.'

Yeah, thought Redpath ironically, a man always was ready to believe a pretty girl in preference to a rough, unshaven backwoodsman. He felt helpless; there was nothing he could do.

Major Leabridge barked an order. 'I will announce your sentence later. Take the prisoner back to the guard cell.'

When he was back behind those bars again, Redpath asked to see Colonel Endricks. The rough-riding, tough-talking colonel didn't stand on ceremony, but came straight down to the guard cell. He growled that he was sorry to see Redpath there on such a charge.

'I didn't send to speak about that,' Redpath said brusquely. 'I'm bein' judged solely upon the word of a girl who probably said a lot of things when she didn't know what she was talkin' about. I reckon she'll feel shame when she hears I am to suffer for it, and she'll stand up and confess. I don't think she's really a bad girl.'

The colonel said, shortly, 'I hope you're right, Redpath. But I won't change my mind until Miss Churl changes it for me. Now what is it you wanted to tell me? Something about them guns?'

'Yes, sir.' Redpath told him the whole story of the finding of the wrecked and abandoned wagon train, and of the chase after the guns.

'So you think a small part of the guns are hidden somewhere around Sweet Water settlement, while the rest are buried close to where the ambush took place?'

'Yes, sir. I haven't mentioned anything of this to Major Leabridge.'

The colonel's head came up at that. 'Oh, why not, Redpath?'

Redpath shrugged cynically. 'What's the good of savin' them guns from one lot of Injuns if the commissioner's only goin' to give 'em to another lot?'

Colonel Endricks kept nodding at that, as if in full sympathy with the sentiment. 'Sure, sure,' he said. 'So nobody apart from yourself knows where them arms is hidden, huh?'

'Apart from the men who stuck up the wagon train, sir. I think you should send an agent down to Sweet Water to keep an eye on the place and see if he can get on to anythin' there, while I'd like to go back an' make a bonfire out of them other arms.'

This time he didn't attempt to hint with his words; he spoke outright because he felt that now the colonel would appreciate straight talking. He did, but he could think of a snag.

'You're a prisoner awaitin' sentence,' he told the hunter

bluntly. 'Someone else will have to go.'

Redpath shrugged. 'By now the sign will have weathered, an' me an' the Pawnees did a lot of ridin' around. I think I could go straight to the place where they're cached, but it'd take a long time for any other man to find it. Even the Pawnees won't know.'

It worried the colonel. 'Goldarn it,' he swore wrathfully. 'What am I to do? I tell you straight, Redpath, though it costs me my commission I won't see them rifies get into Injun hands because of them sentimentalists back in Washington. They've got to be destroyed first, but I can't do that openly.' He looked at Redpath, 'I need a man like you for the job. If the commissioner gets to know what happened to his precious arms he'll demand a troop of cavalry to go out an' bring 'em back under escort. That's the last thing I want to happen.'

'What about Major Leabridge, sir? How will he regard this affair?'

'He's an army man,' barked the colonel. 'He'll think like I do. But don't think he'll forget this case of yours an' let you out to pick up them arms! No, sir! For all we know it might be a trick. Reckon I'd think up some good tricks myself if I were in your position. Still, I'll speak to him.'

He went stamping off, but Redpath didn't feel very optimistic. He couldn't blame the colonel for thinking maybe he was up to some trick to escape punishment.

Within ten minutes, however, the sergeant of the guard announced another visitor. This time the sergeant was a little doubtful of the propriety of leaving them alone under the circumstances, but after a hesitation he withdrew, though reluctantly.

It was Judith. She looked a little pale, but seemed just as calm, just as clear-eyed as ever. He turned eagerly when she came in through that massive wooden door.

'Judith!' he exclaimed in delight. 'Why, I never thought to see you here!'

There was a flash of humour in Judith's dark brown eyes at that. 'I was going to say that of you, Jim!'

Then she came forward a step, her hands suddenly clasping and unclasping nervously. 'Oh, Jim, I just can't believe this of you. It – it can't be true!' Redpath had to turn and look out of the window, suddenly full of emotion. It was a tremendous relief to hear someone say that – that the slander against him wasn't believed. And it was especially welcome, coming from this tall, attractive girl who spoke so quietly, so nice and sensibly . . . so unlike her mistress.

He sighed.

'You don't know how wonderful it is to hear those words, Judith.' He turned, a smile twisting on his face. 'You know, Judith, ever since I came into this awful little cell I've been wonderin' if I'm takin' leave of my senses. I feel so helpless, so incapable of makin' a defence agen the charge. But I'm innocent, Judith, I swear it.'

He told her the whole story, omitting only some of the details regarding the stolen arms. When he had finished she just looked at him and said:

'It's your word against Miss Churl's, Jim.'

Redpath nodded sombrely. 'That's what the major kept tellin' me. Only he prefers to believe a pretty girl, not a rough backwoodsman!' His voice was bitter.

'But I think I'm inclined to believe your story.' He took a quick step forward, his hands reaching to grasp hers, and then he remembered that they were really too near to being strangers for such familiarity and he let his hands drop. But his eyes were shining, nevertheless; it was a tonic to him to hear her words.

There was that note of humour again in her voice as she said: 'Mind you, perhaps it's not so much that I believe you as I don't believe Miss Churl.'

'It's just as good to me,' Redpath said fervently. 'You think you understand why she did it? Because blest if I can.'

'Oh, yes.' She nodded emphatically. 'Girls are funny creatures, Jim,' she smiled. 'Especially girls like Ann Churl.'

She hesitated then went on: 'Perhaps you don't know much about Eastern girls, Jim – how they're brought up, the kind of life they lead back on the east coast.'

'I can imagine it.'

She nodded.

'Girls like Ann have every luxury – they have simply everything they want. Life for them is a round of theatres and parties, with nothing more serious than a decision to be made, possibly several times daily, which clothes to wear.'

Redpath looked at his rough shirt and buckskin trousers and said drily: 'Guess I've been sparin' myself a lot of worries all these years.'

She laughed. 'Yes. She's full of romantic notions, too, Jim, and very, very conceited. She's the kind of girl who must try to secure for herself the most eligible male in any company. And when you responded roughly, perhaps unintentionally, it would produce very mixed feelings inside her.'

He was hardly listening to her words, instead was watching her face as she spoke. She had quite good looks which seemed to grow on him the more he saw her. At first sight Ann Churl might seem the prettier, with her sparkling blue eyes and fair, carefully coiffeured hair, but in little time Redpath had decided that the quieter-dressed companion, Judith, was the fairer flower.

He liked her now because he realized that while apparently being uncomplimentary about her mistress she was yet trying to make excuses for her conduct.

He smiled. 'All right, Judith,' he told her gently. 'I know what you're goin' to say next. You're sayin' the poor gal can't help the way she's been brought up. Well, I say it's a poor way to reward a man who went an' saved her life for her, and the excuse that she didn't know what'n heck she was sayin' when she came ridin' in is pretty thin. She's had time enough since to take back her words.'

'She's sorry she ever said them, Jim, I know,' Judith told him unexpectedly. 'I can feel it when I'm with her; that's what brought me along to see you – feeling sure she had done wrong to you and that therefore you are innocent of this charge.'

This time Redpath took her hands.

'Judith,' he said earnestly, 'won't you go back to her and try to get her to clear me?'

'It won't be easy.' She shook her head doubtfully. 'Especially if she knows I've been to see you, Jim. She's – well, very jealous. She likes to do just the opposite to what I want her to do, at times,' she smiled.

Redpath went back to the barred window and looked out across the parade ground of hard-tramped earth. He said: 'You see that big wagon wheel over by the blacksmith's, Judith?'

She came and looked out from his side. There was an old wheel fixed to a frame up against the wall of the black-smith's workshop. Redpath said: 'The army doesn't keep men in prison as punishment, Judith. They don't like to keep men in idleness an' have others watchin' guard over 'em. There's usually two kinds of punishment.'

Judith's hands fluttered to her throat in horror. 'You mean—?'

'If I don't get shot, that's what I'll get.' His voice was harsh. 'They'll tie me to that wheel, I reckon, stripped to the waist. Then they'll give me fifty lashes – or maybe a hundred because Miss Churl has a mighty pretty face!'

'Oh, Jim!' Her voice was shocked. She could imagine that scene, a public flogging – the pain but also the indignity of it. And she had no doubts now that the punishment would be wrongfully imposed upon an innocent man.

'I'll speak to Miss Churl,' she promised quickly. 'I won't let this happen to you if I can help it.'

'Thanks, Judith.' She crossed to the door and called to the sergeant to let her out. Redpath took her hand and shook it. 'Bless you for believin' in me, Judith. I'll never forget it,' he told her fervently.

She smiled and patted his hand, but he could see she was near to tears. 'Don't worry,' she whispered. 'I'll move heaven and earth. That girl, though – you don't know what a spoilt, peevish child she can be!'

Then the sergeant let her out. Redpath clung to the bars, straining to watch her all the way across to the main block until she passed through a doorway and disappeared from sight. Then he went back to brood alone with his thoughts.

Shortly after his noon-day meal was brought to him, the sergeant of the guard marched in to announce the sentence that had been passed on him.

His first guess had been right. He was to receive fifty lashes. The sentence carried with it a further penalty, however. He was to be discharged from the service of the United States Government as a person unfitted to hold such a position.

'Flogged – then dishonourably dismissed,' he told himself when the sergeant had gone. And meantime, maybe, those arms would be lifted from the cache and passed on to Indians!

CHAPTER EIGHT

THE DANGEROUS MAN

To a man used to freedom, imprisonment even for a few hours was very trying, and most of the time Redpath stood at the small window and watched the never-ceasing activity out on the parade ground.

Always men were going across to the workshops, or were riding through the big gates on missions into the great world outside. Redpath began to see that the colonel's force must be camped outside the fortress, probably a mile or so up the river where the ground was level and gave good grazing to their animals – the fortress was crowded enough as it was with its normal garrison.

Civilians and even friendly Indians came through the gates, sometimes to trade with the soldiers but often merely for an opportunity to exchange conversation.

Suddenly Redpath spotted a familiar face among a group going out through the gates with a light forage cart. It was Lem, one of the men who had been engaged to ride guard on the commissioner's wagons coming up.

'Hey. Lem!' he called. There was a lot he wanted to speak about to the old-timer.

He saw Lem shift and turn in his saddle at sound of his name. Then that scrub-face peered round in his direction.

He saw the eyes light up in recognition under the tattered brim of an old hat, and then Lem frowned and looked away as if not wanting to speak to him.

But Redpath called: 'Can't you speak to a pard, Lem? I never did you no harm.'

The old-timer said something at that to a sergeant who was riding along with the party, then he came cantering over towards the guard-room. He dismounted stiffly and came right up to where Redpath stood at his cell window, and nobody bothered to stop him. Discipline was easy on such occasions, and the sergeant of the guard saw no harm in a prisoner having words with a friend.

Redpath saw that Lem was uneasy and didn't want to look him in the face. So he said:

'That's all right, old-timer. I never did anythin' to that gal, an' right now Miss Judith's sure tryin' to get her to undo her mischief.'

'Miss Judith?' The old-timer's eyes looked at him with interest at that.

'Sure. She came to see me, Lem. She believes me. She knows it's just a trumped-up story from an hysterical female.'

Lem sighed. 'I sure hope Miss Judith does clear you. I never did quite believe it, Jim. You don't look a man of that kind. Still, what are you to believe when you see a frightened, cryin' female sayin' she's been attacked an' then sayin' you had a, hand in it?'

'That's all right, Lem. I don't blame anyone for thinkin' the way they did.' He paused, eyeing the old man queerly through the bars. 'That sure was the strangest hold-up I ever experienced, Lem.'

Lem stopped chewing. 'How come, Jim?'

'For six Injuns to stampede fourteen or fifteen white men.'

Lem began on his tobacco again. He didn't speak for some time, and when he did it was to ask a question. It was as if there was a lot on his mind, but whether he spoke about it or not depended largely upon the hunter's answer.

'Six Injuns? What makes you say six, Jim? I'd have said maybe more.'

'I went over the place afterwards, Lem. The ambush was started by six 'breeds or Injuns. I don't know which. Six Injuns threw a powerful scare into you.'

Lem seemed to take a deep breath. 'Jim, I don't mind tellin' you I've lain awake every night since tryin' to figger out that stick-up. It sure was the queerest thing I ever heard tell of.'

He came and stood against the cell wall and spoke earnestly about the holdup. 'Maybe if I told you what happened, you'll see more to it than I did. I'm foxed, Jim. We was goin' nice an' steadily along, only a day's march from Fort Phil. We came to a place just right for an ambush, though I reckon I wasn't thinkin' of such things at the time.

'I was ridin' about fifty yards ahead of the leadin' wagon, with Darky, Luke and another feller right behind me. The rest of the men was strung all along the wagon line an' behind it, I reckon.

'Wal, suddenly I heard a shout from Darky, an' I turned an' saw him fall out of the saddle. There was an arrow stickin' out of him. And when I looked back down the line, holy nuggets, but nearly every saddle was empty! 'Cept for we few right up in front they'd wiped out nearly every man with that first volley.'

He paused, and his fading grey eyes looked past him into the darkness of that small cell. He was thinking back to those moments when he had lost his pard.

Then his eyes jerked back to Redpath's face.

'I reckon a dozen fell at that first volley, pretty near – Darky, every blamed teamer, Mick Culhedy, Jep Connor, Joe Loup an' Rupe Riarn. I never seed any of 'em after that. So you'll kinda see my doubts when you say six Injuns only was behind that stick-up.'

Redpath was astonished. 'That's the queerest story—' he began. His eyes grew thoughtful. He was ready to swear that no more than six men had lain in ambush on the wagon train, and in corroboration was the fact that the Pawnees were all agreed on that, too.

So he said: 'I tell you, Lem, six men only was waitin' there for you.'

Lem spat in disgust. 'Six men couldn't have shot down a dozen in one volley, Jim. It isn't possible – unless they used both arms at once!'

They stared at each other through the little window. Then Redpath said slowly: 'It's queer, Lem, mighty queer. But isn't that what you said when you first started to talk about it?' Lem nodded, chewing vigorously. 'Well, you tell me what struck you as queer about the raid.'

'I reckon everythin' was queer,' Lem said. 'That was the first time we didn't have scouts ridin' well in front. The first time we don't have scouts, we walk slap bang into an ambush. That's queer, ain't it?'

Redpath nodded. 'Joe Loup was wagonmaster. He's not the kind to take risks normally.'

Lem shrugged and changed the subject. 'Next thing seemed mighty queer was the way everyone went down without more than just one yell from poor old Darky.'

'They didn't?'

'Nope. Now I figger it ain't often a dozen men gets killed so neatly they don't let out more'n one yawp . . . Darky's.'

Redpath was staring at him. He'd never been in a fight like that, either. Rarely did a man get killed instantaneously from an arrow wound, in his experience.

'What happened after that, Lem?' he asked.

'We hadn't time to circle the wagons. Besides, we had no men left to defend 'em. An' the Injuns started to shoot down the wagon hosses an' mules. There were five of us on hosses. I shouted to Luke to go hole up in a gully just a way ahead. It looked a good place if you had your back to the wall – an' we had.

'I rode back to the commissioner's wagon. He'd fallen out of the wagon when his teamer was killed. I told him to run like hell fer the gully, but give the devil his due, he wouldn't go without his womenfolk.' He spat at that.

Evidently he hadn't expected such conduct from an Easterner and an Indian agent.

'Well, we got 'em all across, though that Miss Ann was screamin' with hysterics. I reckon it had come a bit quick, follerin' things the previous day.' Then he shut up, realizing he was back on dangerous ground.

'It's strange – they shot down so many with the first volley,' Redpath said, 'yet they let you get those people safely away from the first wagon.'

Lem sighed. 'Everythin's plumb crazy about that blamed raid. I saw Injuns come on to the trail right back of the wagons. Maybe they was so consarned with lootin' they forgot about us.'

'But they didn't try to smoke you out, Lem?'

'Nope. Queerest Injuns I've ever seen, Jim. A couple of 'em came right up to see what's what, but when we fired a few times they nipped out of sight right smartly an' went back to lootin' the wagons.' Again he sighed. 'You know, pard, I got an idea they only intended ter hurt us if we came out an' got awkward.'

'So you lay up in that gully an' watched the train being looted, then when they went away you doubled up an' came ridin' in to Fort Phil?'

Lem nodded. Redpath looked out on to the parade ground, now full of men going across to the cookhouse. He saw Running Bear and the other wounded Pawnee walk across with the soldiers. They seemed little worse for their wounds, though the second Pawnee limped as he walked.

Redpath's eyes came back to the old-timer. 'Lem, how many bodies d'you reckon we found at the ambush?'

Lem blinked and stopped chewing. 'Reckon it'd be around twelve. There'd be Darky, the Smith boy—'

Redpath interrupted. 'We found seven.'

'I told you that was the queerest raid, Jim,' Lem complained. 'Everythin' about it was queer.'

'It sure was,' said the hunter grimly. 'But I'm beginnin' to see daylight now. We never found the bodies of Joe Loup,

Riarn, Connor and Mick Culhedy. Did Stuart an' Morg Day ride in with you?'

'Nope. They went down in the ambush, too.'

'It's queer,' the hunter said significantly. 'I didn't find their bodies, either!'

'Mebbe the wolves had got at 'em. They sent a party off as soon as we got in next mornin', an' they reported most o' the corpses pretty badly mauled. They reckoned some must have been dragged away in the bush, because they couldn't account fer all our men.'

'Joe Loup sure had it all figgered out!' Redpath said unexpectedly.

So Lem asked: 'What's on your mind, Jim?'

The hunter spoke slowly. 'I'm beginnin' to think Joe Loup's behind all this raid. When he heard of the guns and ammunition he probably figgered on makin' a fortune in trade if he could lay hands on 'em. I reckon he sent one of his pards ahead to fix an ambush with some people he knew up in Sweet Water.'

'Injuns?'

'I guess not. I reckon we'll find they are 'breeds, like Joe. Maybe related to him. They dressed up like Injuns so as to throw us off their scent, but their scheme kinda fell to pieces because I came on the scene within hours of the raid – before any wolves could have got away with any bodies.

'I know Joe Loup an' his pards aren't lyin' there dead, so it shows they were up to somethin' in fallin' off their hosses as they did. It's mighty queer that the six fellars you saw come off their mounts was Joe an' his particular pards, huh?'

Lem looked at him, then spat. 'I sure said it was a blamed queer raid,' he told him.

There was silence for a while, both men busy with their thoughts. Then Lem spoke again. 'I was goin' out with a party to fetch in them broken wagons, but mebbe I'll stay around Fort Phil instead.'

Redpath said, 'Oh, why?'

'I figger mebbe Miss Judith won't get that skittish young filly to go back on anything she's said. If so, mebbe you might need someone when it's all over.'

For some reason it hadn't occurred to the hunter that Judith might fail to get her mistress to retract. Now his jaw tightened, looking across at that wagon wheel by the smithy.

'You don't think so?'

Lem shook his head regretfully. 'I reckon it comes hard to a gal to eat her own words. It needs a mighty big woman to do a thing like that, I guess. Now, that Miss Ann – she ain't big in any way, though maybe the other gal has got more in her. Nope, I reckon every time they go to talk to her she'll throw a whole lot more hysterics.'

Redpath's heart sank. Again he looked across at that worn old wheels Then he said, teeth gritted, 'I never did it, an' I won't let 'em put a lash on me if I can help it.'

Lem said, 'That's why I figgered on stayin' around, Jim. I reckoned it might come to that.'

Redpath stared at him. 'Come to what, old-timer? Speak plain, can't you?'

'Ain't you figgerin' on bustin' outa gaol, then?' Lem spoke cautiously now, in case anyone was around the corner. He said, 'Goldarn it, in your place I would, Jim. An' you c'n bet I'll help you. I won't stand by an' see an innocent man whipped.'

Redpath was touched. 'Thanks,' he said. 'But I won't get you into trouble. Helpin' me bust outa gaol could end with you standin' where I am instead.'

Lem rubbed his stubble with a baccy-stained thumb. 'You figger how to get outa gaol, Jim. I'll have your hoss ready waitin' fer you if you c'n make it. Reckon I'll ride out with it now, in fact, an' leave it where some oaks run right into the river, a quarter-mile back along the trail. I'll put up some food an' ammunition for you, an' leave a rifle in the boot. There's a new Sharps repeater I might lay my hands on.'

Redpath drew in his breath quickly. 'Lem, if you c'n do all that for me. . . .'

Lem said, 'I'd hand you a gun, too, right now, only they'd see me reachin' up to the window with it, I reckon. If you need a gun, you'll have to get that yourself.'

Redpath said, 'I'll never be able to thank you enough, Lem,' but the old-timer cut him short.

'Somebody's comin'. Goldarn it, it looks like the commissioner hissel'.'

He said no more, but with a brief nod he walked to the rail where his mount was hitched. As he rode back towards the garrison stables, a new figure came into view. It was Henry Churl.

Redpath drew back from the window, not wanting to see the man, but a few seconds later he realized that Churl was coming to visit him. He was certainly having plenty of visitors that day, he thought grimly.

The sergeant shouted for him to come to attention, and then Churl walked in, very pompous, very smooth in his fine city clothes – big and heavy and the picture of stern authority. The sergeant and one man armed with a rifle stayed with them in the cell. Evidently Redpath was to be regarded as a dangerous malefactor, so far as the commissioner was concerned.

A wild hope had leapt into Redpath's breast when he realized that the commissioner was coming in to see him. His thoughts were: 'Judith's been successful! Ann has confessed and now her father has come to make apology!'

But those hopes were dashed the moment he saw that fat, stern face. He knew Henry Churl wasn't there for that reason.

He waited in silence, just looking at the portly commissioner. After an uncertain pause, Henry Churl said sternly, 'You repaid my hospitality in a fine way, Redpath.'

'Your daughter might be able to alter that opinion, commissioner.'

A fat hand lifted and waved impatiently. 'I have been told you are accusing my daughter of inventing the story.' He grew indignant. 'My daughter has been brought up to honour the truth, Redpath. She is incapable of any act of

84

meanness or of telling a lie, and I will not hear such things said against her.'

Redpath was silent at that, not because he was intimidated but for another reason. Whatever his follies this portly man thought the world of his daughter; a pang smote Redpath's heart to think of the pain that must come to this fond, indulgent parent if ever the truth came out.

Commissioner Churl lifted his plump chin and said, 'I want you to know, Redpath, that though you planned to do harm to my daughter she has begged that you should not be made to suffer from the lash as the major intends. You should give thanks for that piece of generosity and forgiveness, Redpath, even though it has failed to move the commander in the slightest.'

So pretty Ann Curl, probably horrified to learn of the trouble she was bringing on her rescuer, had tried to intercede on his behalf with the major – and failed. Well, he thought, if she just opened her mouth and spoke the truth he would find it in him to admire her more than he did right now!

He still said nothing. The commissioner looked at him as if he were something completely beyond redemption. It was plain that he, at any rate, was touched by his daughter's apparently noble action.

When it became obvious that the stony-faced hunter did not intend to speak, the commissioner broached the subject of the trainload of arms.

'I'm told that you rode off with a band of Pawnee scouts to try to recover those arms,' he said. 'I can't find out the result of your mission.'

Redpath spoke politely. 'I have made my report to Colonel Endricks. If you want the information you should go an' ask him for it.'

Churl gestured. 'Unfortunately the colonel's out with the party surveying the new road.'

'The Bozeman Trail?' asked the hunter quickly. This confirmed his guess.

Before he realized what he was doing the commissioner

nodded. Then he asked, 'Didn't you know that's why they sent the troops up here? To build the road during late fall when the Indians would be too occupied with hunting winter food, and their ponies were lean because the grasses are thin and dry.' He spoke bitterly, like a man who feels he is being let down everywhere.

Redpath's eyes twinkled. It must have been galling. Here the peacemakers back in Washington were offering the redman freedom in the Big Horn mountains, while not many yards away the War Department was projecting a new road to Montana where the big new goldfields were – planning it to run bang through the Big Horn country! It was typical of government departments, the left hand never knowing what the right hand was doing.

The Bozeman Trail was nothing new. Pioneers, braving the perils of the Indian country, had made this rough trail in their efforts to reach the scene of the fabulous gold strikes around Virginia City. The United States Government, impoverished by the recent Civil War, badly needed that gold, ands now it seemed they were determined to ensure that it could be brought safely out through the Indian country.

If the road was to be built by the army it would be a military road, with forts stationed all along its course to give adequate protection to the traffic on it. It was a good scheme, to plan to build it in the fall, when game was scarcer and the Indians had to concern themselves more with hunting than with war. In spring they would probably have proved too troublesome to the road-builders and even if it had been successfully completed it would only have been accomplished at a terrible cost of human life, white and red.

Redpath began to understand now why his friend Captain Riddell and Colonel John Endricks were so concerned at the thought of five hundred rifles and a few tons of ammunition being placed in the hands of Big Horn tribes.

Rifles meant more successful hunting; easier hunting

meant the release of many braves to fight the invader of their rich hunting grounds – and they would fight with those same rifles that had been given them.

Redpath sighed. It was all very simple, now that the secret was known to him. Well, Commissioner Churl's Indians weren't going to get any rifles if he could avoid it.

Churl spoke sharply: 'Well?'

Redpath said, 'You're the last man on earth I'd make my report to, commissioner.'

Churl's chin came up. Like a lot of fat men he had plenty of fighting spirit, even though he did not always fight wisely.

'Why?'

'Because', said Redpath contemptuously, 'only a blamed fool and an Easterner would go give an Injun a breech-loadin' Henry. Why, they're better guns than a lot of these muzzle-loadin' Martins the infantry's got out here. Hand five hundred rifles to the local redmen an' you'll kill five hundred men on that Bozeman Trail before it reaches Virgini' City, Commissioner. Didn't anyone ever tell you that, back in Washington?'

Churl's fat lips compressed. 'You should stick to your job, Redpath, and leave me and the Indian Office to ours. We know better than you.'

'What do you know?' Redpath challenged. He moved forward aggressively as he spoke, and that brought the guard up with his rifle.

'I know that we could buy peace in this country if we gave the redman good guns so that he wouldn't want for food. His buffalo herds are thinning, and he finds it difficult now to get sufficient game with his primitive bows and arrows. We think that if we give him good guns he'll be happy, and our theory is that only starving, unhappy warriors go to war.'

Redpath looked at him in disgust. He thought, 'The blamed idlot really believes this. He doesn't realize that fightin' is part of an Injun's code of honour – he's got to kill someone or else none of the girls will look twice at him.

And he won't fight until his belly is full!'

But what was the good of arguing against Eastern inexperience? The bureaucrats in Washington were always sure
they knew better than the people on the spot.

He glanced at the veteran army sergeant, a man who
must have fought the Indians all across the Plains, and it
seemed to him that the professionally wooden face yet
held a glimmer that could be a mirror of his own
contempt.

He said ironically, 'I'd have thought you'd have changed
your mind after your recent troubles with Injuns.'

'I don't change my mind,' snapped the commissioner.
'The way Indians are treated around here, you can expect
some hotheads to raid wagon trains. The Indian agent here
tells me that it's the first time he's ever heard of an Indian
Commissioner's wagons being robbed. He says if they'd
known who was coming in on the trail, no Indian would
have lifted a hand against me.'

'Sure,' drawled Redpath caustically. 'Why rob the
commissioner when they know he's goin' to give them the
stuff anyway?' He didn't tell him that the raid in any event
had not been conducted by hostile Indians, as Churl apparently supposed.

The commissioner got impatient. 'Well, aren't you going
to tell me anything about your search?'

'Nothin',' said the hunter coolly.

'Because you're in trouble over my daughter?' challenged Churl.

'No – because you're a dangerous man, though you'll be
the last to believe it.'

'Pah!' Then Churl said, with heavy cunning, 'Suppose I
speak and get your sentence reduced?'

Redpath looked at him contemptuously. 'You're
kiddin'! You wouldn't do that. So stop tryin' to bluff me. If
I'm to be flogged at the wheel, all right, I'll be flogged and
that's all there is to it.'

He thought he heard a sound outside at that. It sounded
like a gasp – a woman's voice. And when he heard it he

knew that Judith had failed to get Ann Churl to retract on the wild statements she had made against him!

CHAPTER NINE

JIM'S MISSION

He spoke again. A little louder this time. 'Give me a gun and I won't stay to be flogged, I promise you.'

The sergeant's voice suddenly broke in on their talk. 'You'll get no gun while I'm on guard, Redpath.'

Churl nodded approvingly. 'You'll have to take your medicine, Redpath. You deserve it, and I'm only sorry that it is my daughter who is responsible for your getting your true deserts.'

'Commissioner, you talk like a humbug.' Redpath had had enough of this conversation. 'Go back east, where you'll be on familiar ground, but don't come out here with your sanctimonious talk. It cuts no ice with me, an' even less with your red friends.'

Commissioner Churl was indignant. Rarely was he addressed in such a manner. But Redpath contemptuously turned his back on him and showed that he had no intention of taking part in any further conversation. So Churl, with an angry, muttered exclamation, suddenly wheeled and propelled his portly body out through the cell door.

It thudded to, and he heard the locks go on and the steel bolts shoot across. He sat down to wait.

When it was coming dusk Judith came to see him. She didn't stay long. She said simply, 'It wasn't any good, Jim. She just ran away from me, weeping, every time I tried to speak for you.' She reached out and took his hand. 'Jim, I know by the way she's behaving now that she's in the wrong. If it's any consolation, that girl's suffering, Jim!'

He shrugged. However much he tried, his own peril kept him from feeling sympathy with the author of all his present troubles. He had seen men lashed more than once. He remembered a camp cook down at Palo Duro who had sold a gun to an Indian. They had flogged that cook spread-eagled across a wheel, just as he would be flogged tomorrow at dawn. The man's back was a mass of raw flesh for days afterwards, and he was unable to do anything but lie around in the shade for a week at least because of the agony that movement would bring. To this day the man's back would be a criss-cross pattern of ridged scars.

And he had received only thirty lashes!

He thought, 'If they give me fifty, then I'll never be able to get down to them guns that's cached before Joe Loup an' his pals sneak back to get 'em.'

But even while he was thinking of it, Judith was slipping a Colt .45 into his hand. She had understood his message all right!

'Goodbye and good luck,' she whispered, turning to go. 'Probably we'll never meet again, Jim, but I'm not sorry I've known you even for so short a time.

That was what he liked about this girl. She didn't go coy and arch in her speech with a man. She said what she thought, and it sounded no less modest and ladylike for all that. He smiled his gratefulness. 'If I can, we'll meet again,' he promised. 'Just you keep at Miss Ann, an' then maybe I'll be able to ride into Fort Phil again with my head high.'

When Judith had gone he sat down to make his plans. He was determined to escape if at all possible rather than tamely submit to a frightful flogging, and he knew that any man in his position, guilty or innocent, would do likewise. Well, he had a gun and his guards didn't know that, and if he were smart he might use it to turn the tables on them.

It was a risky business, but then Jim Redpath's whole life was bounded by risk.

He decided that his best chance would be to escape

when they brought his supper. It would be approaching dark then, and the fortress gates would be closed very soon afterwards. Dusk would screen his movements and help him to escape.

But, as always happens, things didn't go quite according to normal routine that evening. For some reason, though the supper bugle blew on time, the guard was late in bringing the prisoner his food.

He stood in agony at the window and watched the dark of evening descend. Up on the look-out tower above the gate he felt the restlessness as the sentries waited for the order to close the massive palisade doors for the night. Time was speeding away, and with every minute that passed his chances of getting out of the fortress that night diminished.

Then, to his relief, he heard growling voices outside his cell door, heard keys jangle on a ring and the padlocks come unfastened one by one. Hastily he went across to his wooden bed and sat on it.

The guard came in with his supper. Outside, Redpath knew, another sentry, armed with a rifle, would be standing.

But only one guard came in. When that man lifted his eyes he found himself looking into the muzzle of a blue-barrelled Colt.

Redpath didn't say a word. He just sat behind his gun and left it to the guard to decide what he wanted. The guard wasn't dumb. He gulped twice very quickly, then slowly put down his food cans and then elevated his arms.

The hunter nodded with satisfaction. He rose and pushed the door rather more closed, then whispered, 'Out of that tunic – quick!'

His Colt lifted suggestively. The guard came apart from his tunic in record time. Redpath fixed a gag in the man's mouth with a neck cloth that the guard was wearing under his tunic, then tied his wrists together with the man's own belt. Not satisfied, he then fastened the man's feet to the leg of his bed, which was nailed securely down into the wooden flooring. That would prevent any drumming of heels which might draw too early attention to his plight.

The hunter then put on the tunic, buttoned it to the neck, as the guard had been wearing it, then put on the long-peaked cap.

The sentry outside was too bored to look closely at the guard who came shuffling backwards out of the cell. Within minutes his turn of duty would end, and just then he could think of nothing better than the delights of a night in bed.

He heard the padlocks go on, and the jangle of keys as they came out and clinked together on the solid steel ring. Then the guard walked past him, rubbing his cheek with his hand as if testing the growth of his beard. At the time he had an idle thought that a man should not be so badly in need of a shave after only twenty-four hours on guard. But then his mind went blank again, and he forgot the trivial circumstance.

Redpath breathed a sigh of relief when he was safely past the lounging sentry outside the cell door. He was out on a veranda which ended in some three or four wooden steps down to the parade ground in front of the guardroom. Thirty yards away were the gates.

And those gates were being closed as Redpath came down on to the parade ground.

Someone called to him as he started across to the gates. It was the sergeant of the guard, but he neither knew it nor cared. In a quarter of a minute those gates would be barred for the night, and then he would be a prisoner within the fortress.

He walked briskly across to the four men who were straining steadily to keep the massive gates moving. Perhaps they thought he was a good-natured comrade coming to give them a hand.

He came up, then bent and pushed, head down between his arms, just as they were shoving. Then, when the gates were only a yard apart, he slipped between them. A second later the doors came to with a mighty thud, and with a sense of exhilaration he realized that he was free.

True there would still be one sentry on watch above, but

he stood a chance of escaping observation with dusk so far upon them.

He was just starting away from the gates when he heard an exclamation from inside. 'Goldarn it, I could have swore someone came out ter give us a hand just now!'

Then another bewildered voice, 'What'n the tarnation, there was someone—'

But Redpath sped swiftly away into the gathering darkness, not interested in the outcome of their astonished reactions to his disappearance. He knew that within minutes it was likely that the supper-guard's absence from the guardroom would be noticed, but provided Lem had left him his horse as he had promised, then he had little fear of pursuit now.

He was away. Admittedly he was now something of an outlaw, and would have to avoid army camps in future. But at least he would be spared that frightful and quite unmerited flogging, and beyond that he could think of nothing else.

As he ran swiftly down the trail towards the bend where the trees were, he heard no sound from behind other than the normal life of the barracks. It all seemed too easy, the way he had escaped. Then he patted the gun which he had stuffed inside his tunic. King Colt often made things easy for a man.

A horse was picketed among the trees, just as Lem had said. And it was his own horse. When it recognized Redpath, it whinnied and nuzzled up to him in delight, and Redpath patted the soft nose and murmured his own pleasure in return.

He felt around in the darkness under the trees, and his exploring fingers discovered a full pack behind the saddle, a belt of ammunition and a rifle in the boot. That rifle interested him. He had never owned a Sharps repeater before, but by the feel of it, he owned one now!

He wondered where Lem had acquired it and why he had given him such a valuable present. Perhaps it was the man's good-hearted attempt to compensate him for the injustice that had been done, and must continue to be done, against him while he rode the trails alone, an outlaw.

He swung into his saddle, then remembered the blue army tunic he was wearing. He stripped it off and dropped it to the ground, then threw the ring of keys after it. He didn't know how they'd release the guard now until daylight came and they were able to find those keys.

He pulled out on to the trail, then again paused to listen. He thought he heard some excitement back inside the fort, but he could have been mistaken. Taking no chances, he put spurs to his mount and rode hell for leather down the trail while there was yet any light to see by.

His object was to put as great a distance as possible between him and the fortress and so avoid any trouble, but in fact he merely rode right into it.

Less than half a mile along the track he ran into a bunch of riders returning to the fortress. He had a momentary, startled impression of Indian faces around him, then managed to recognize his friend, Captain Riddell, among them. The Pawnees were returning from their scouting expedition.

Everyone abruptly sat back on their horses and there was a great commotion of flying hoofs and scared, tossing horses' heads. When it subsided Riddell called, 'Hallo, Reddy, where do you think you're off to?' And at that the hunter realized that his friend had no knowledge of the charge against him or of the fact that he had been held a prisoner.

He didn't enlighten him. As an officer Riddell was unorthodox, but all the same Redpath knew he would take him in charge back to the fortress if he knew that he, Redpath, was an escaped prisoner.

So he said, 'I'm just goin' down the trail a piece.' But he didn't say why and Riddell didn't think to ask him. Anyway, Riddell was much too interested in the fate of those wagon-loads of guns to be bothered by anything else at that moment.

Briefly Redpath outlined the story for him, including his

suspicions of Joe Loup's instigation of the affair. All the time he was alert for sounds of pursuit from behind, but so far none came.

'So you think Loup's got part of the load hidden away at the Sweet Water settlement, while most of it is cached quite near to the scene of the stick-up?'

'Yes. I think I know where that cache is, too,' Redpath told him. 'I won't tell you where it is, because then it would be your duty as an officer to collect those guns and hand them over to the commissioner. I've spoken to Henry Churl today, an' I c'n tell you he's as dead set as ever on given' them guns to the Injuns.'

'If he does that, now,' he heard Riddell say softly, 'it'll be the end of the new Bozeman Trail this year.'

Redpath looked up. 'You mean—'

'This territory is alive with Injuns. The secret's out, Reddy. Somehow the Injuns have got to know about the buildin' of a new road through their territory, an' they're massing in strength, determined to stop it. That explains why the Dog Soldiers are so far from their Platte huntin' grounds. The whole Cheyenne tribe has moved up with them, too, and I wouldn't be surprised to find there's Sioux an' Blackfoot, Snakes, Crows an' Comanches pullin' into the country.'

He leaned forward earnestly. 'Reddy, if them guns fall into these Injuns' hands at this time, it'll be a massacre every time we start out to build that road. Men can't work an' fight at the same time – they certainly can't do it agen rifles as good as their own.'

'Better,' said Redpath, remembering some of the muzzle-loading Martins he had seen among the infantry. 'All right, Bob, I'll do my darndest. But now it's pretty tough – I'm workin' on my own.'

Riddell didn't understand, but Redpath wasn't going to explain further. He was listening very intently now, for he thought he had detected the sounds of approaching horse-men.

He wheeled his horse. 'So long, cap'n,' he called. 'I'm

on my way now.' And he went off into the darkness like a
rocket. Half a minute later Captain Riddell's troop was challenged by a strong party of cavalry from the fortress. Then
he understood why Redpath had left him so abruptly.

'Assault a girl?' Riddell swore. 'Redpath would never do
a thing like that!' And he mentally wished the hunter good
luck in whatever enterprise he was following. He decided
not to mention to anyone the little item of information that
Redpath had given him – that the big cache of arms was
close to where the wagon train had been robbed. For he
figured that maybe that was where Redpath was heading
right then.

He was. He came down to a trot, once away from the
Pawnee scouts, and as he rode through the night he specu-
lated upon the irony of things. Here he was, outlawing
himself in an effort to avoid savage punishment from the
United States soldiery, yet his first action on finding his
freedom was to ride in an effort to save the lives of those
soldiers – he was on his way to destroy guns which might fall
into enemy hands.

All through the night he rode, anxious to get into position by that cache before Joe Loup and his renegades could
return. He had no real plan for when he got there, but at
least if he were on the spot he might be able to put a stop
to their little activities, one way or another.

At one stage of his journey he proceeded with extra
caution, for he knew that the party which had left Fort Phil
to bring in the broken wagons must be camping somewhere
across the trail. Because it was a small party he guessed they
would be camping without fires, and that made things very
difficult for him.

Luck was with him. As he came over a soft part of the
trail he heard a horse's nostrils blow out as it paused while
cropping grass. He guessed he had found the party, and he
walked his horse off the trail and made a wide circuit before
returning to it again.

Shortly after dawn he arrived at the scene of the hold-up.
The wagons were still there, but he thought there were

further signs of looting. Probably some wandering hunting party had come across them and had helped themselves. If that were so, if some Indians had found such abandoned treasures on the trail, then it was certain they would return in force at an early opportunity to secure the rest.

It made things very difficult for him. Lying in wait for a party of renegades was one thing, but trying to hide up in the middle of a swarm of looting Indians was quite another!

However, there was nothing the hunter could do about it, so his next move was to go and explore the place behind that grove of trees where he suspected the arms had been buried. He rode round, to come upon the place from behind, because he had no wish to leave fresh tracks which might arouse the suspicions of the renegades when they returned. On the edge of the clearing he dismounted and walked across the trampled ground.

He guessed that a hole had been dug to receive the surplus weapons and boxes of ammunition before the ambush was set on the wagon train, in anticipation of more loot than they could carry. Otherwise the looters could not have gone through their work and got away so quickly, he thought.

Now he could see faint traces of digging – the place had a yellower look than the surrounding ground, not altogether accounted for by the churning action of many sharp hoofs. Walking the horses up and down the clearing had been effective in disguising the digging operations at the time, but now that suspicion was directed against the place there were unmistakable clues as to what had happened.

But having found the place, as he was now pretty certain he had, he was at a loss what next to do.

He couldn't set to work and dig out the arms and ammunition, because in this country a man needed to be vigilant, and a man digging could never be that. Besides, it was hardly likely that he would get far if he tried to dispose of several tons of arms unaided.

So he decided to lie up and perhaps go into action when Joe Loup and his friends sneaked back for another load. He had a feeling they wouldn't stay away long, because the next shower of rain would probably damage the buried weapons.

He returned to his horse, mounted and went climbing back a half-mile to where a pine belt started on the steep hillside. There he hid his faithful horse in the darkness of the close-set, straight-trunked trees, and then he clambered across to a point which gave cover and yet permitted a wide view across the trail.

For several hours he lay there, his keen eyes continually roaming the wooded hill country all around him, his thoughts busy on alternative plans for disposing of the stolen arms.

His best bet, he decided, was to let Joe Loup and his renegades obligingly dig the loot up out of the soil, and then, at the point of his gun, force them to destroy the arms and ammunition themselves. Once get those cartridges burning and the flare-up would destroy any amount of guns in no time.

Redpath had to chuckle at the thought of it. Joe Loup would suffer agonies at being made to destroy what he and his followers had so cunningly sought to get for themselves.

It was a plan full of dangers and hazards, but Redpath felt that he could pull it off successfully. He patted his new Sharps repeater lovingly. With this fine new weapon he felt that he could tackle half a dozen or even a dozen train robbers and stand more than an even chance of getting away with it.

Early in the afternoon there was a stir along the trail. As he watched from his vantage, high above it, he saw the recovery party from Fort Phil come trotting up with the spare horses to take away the wagons. They had one wagon with them, probably containing spare wheels to replace those wantonly damaged by Joe Loup's friends.

They worked for over an hour to get those wagons mobile again, and Redpath, even from that distance, felt that they were working at high pressure, anxious to be away from this dangerous country.

Then came the moment when the led horses were

hitched into the traces and the wagons pulled away, surrounded by a small cavalcade of soldiers. Redpath watched them roll out of sight, then continued to watch the dust haze that rose higher than the trees that screened the distant length of the trail. Then even that was lost in the distance.

And Joe Loup didn't come that day.

Next morning a party of well-mounted cavalry went loping by below him, probably on their way with despatches to the nearest telegraph station at North Platte. Then nothing else happened until late in the afternoon.

Redpath was feeling very weary of his vigil by this time, and was wondering if in fact Joe Loup would return as he anticipated. He was tempted now to get on his horse and ride right out of the country – maybe circle round and strike the trail for the new cattle country that was opening up on the Texas plains. By all accounts a man could forget his past there, and he had always hankered after running a ranch of his own—

Abruptly his weariness vanished. Far across the valley he had caught a movement among the trees. His eyes narrowed against the bright sunlight – and that movement came again.

Then someone came riding cautiously out into the open, about a couple of hundred yards up the trail from the scene of the wagon hold-up.

An Indian!

Redpath watched while other Indians came out to join him. They were nearly naked, and because of that he guessed that these would be his old enemies, the Dog Soldiers. At this time of the year, with autumn evenings growing perceptibly chilly, most Indians hereabouts would be wearing shirts and breeches. Only a Spartan warrior band like the Dog Soldiers would disdain such comforts.

These were evidently scouts, and when they were satisfied they came cantering down towards the place where the broken wagons had lain on the dusty track. When they were fifty yards or so on to the trail, more Indians began to ride out after them.

Redpath was startled. Almost it seemed as though they would never stop riding out! In all he thought there must be close on a hundred warriors in the party.

Then he saw the prisoners. There were two of them, and by the way they swayed in their saddles they seemed to have had a bad time. And these weren't Indians, either – they were white men.

The hunter watched them with interest as they rode down the trail – but when they turned off it and rode directly up to that clearing in the grove where the buried loot was, his interest turned to astonishment.

The prisoners were close up with the leaders now, and clearly were pointing out the site to the exultant Indians. When they were there, a dozen or more braves at once jumped down and with their hands began to dig quickly into the soft earth. Within minutes their efforts were rewarded. High above them, Redpath saw a case dragged to the surface – saw it opened with savage blows from a toma-hawk, and half a dozen rifles revealed.

He could sense the delight from the warriors at this success, and now the digging operations were resumed with frantic haste.

Box after box of weapons were dragged forth. At first they were broken open and the contents distributed among the delighted warriors, but when all had been served out with a weapon the remaining cases were left intact and instead were put in front of riders who immediately set off slowly, balancing their heavy, clumsy burdens, and retracing their steps into the hills beyond.

It took a surprisingly short time for the cache to be unearthed and the contents disposed of. But in that time Redpath had decided he knew who those two white prison-ers were – two of the white renegades, Morg Day and Rupe Riarn.

And he began to understand the situation. A second expedition by the renegades to bring in the stolen arms had run into the Dog Warriors. Perhaps Day and Riarn were the only two survivors, and they had tried to buy their freedom by promising to lead the Indians to where the arms and ammunition were buried.

Then Redpath's thoughts switched to another track. The digging had ceased; now the horses were loading up and departing.

But all the boxes recovered so far were arms cases. No ammunition had come to light, and the Indians were riding away as if not expecting to find any.

Redpath couldn't understand it. All he could think was that perhaps the ammunition had been hidden separately from the weapons and for some reason the renegades hadn't disclosed the whereabouts of the second cache.

He watched the line of horsemen turn off the trail and disappear slowly into the cover on the far hillside. He thought grimly, but would Day and Riarn keep their mouths closed about that other valuable cache?

He hoped to heaven they would! Losing the rifles to the Indians was a bitter blow, but in fact those rifles for the moment weren't much good to the Indians until they could find ammunition for them.

He rose to his feet. He knew he must get word through to his friend, Captain Riddell, to warn him that the Indian opposition had been potentially strengthened by the acquisition of those five hundred Henry rifles. But more than that he felt he must find and destroy that ammunition and thus prevent it from falling into the hands of the Dog Warriors.

He rode down to the scene of the recent excavations, hoping that in some way he might tumble upon the secret of the second cache, but the moment he saw the confusion of new-turned soil and trampled earth his heart sank. If the ammunition was buried here, then it was effectually hidden from him. It would need a hundred men with spades and shovels to dig up all that clearing.

He mounted again, after kicking around in the dirt for a while, and this time he took the trail after the Dog Soldiers.

Day and Riarn knew the secret of the missing ammunition. He was going to try to get it from them before the Indians got the information.

CHAPTER TEN

ANN AGAIN!

The trail was easy to follow, but Redpath made no haste to catch up with the Dog Soldiers. He could do nothing while they were on the move, and would have to see what could be done when he discovered their camp.

It took all of two hours for the heavily-laden warriors to return to their camp, in the hills close to the Powder River. Redpath saw it from a high point in the trail – a village of tepees, each band of the tribe having its own circle of lodges, and there were eighteen circles and about ten to twelve tepees in each ring.

Redpath calculated from that that there would be about four hundred Dog Warriors in camp here. That was a formidable party to face, in addition to all the other Indian tribes who were reported to be moving into the area. Himself, Redpath would far rather face half a dozen Indians – even the fighting Cheyennes – than one savage Dog Warrior.

Having discovered the whereabouts of the camp, he rode with even greater caution, never moving from cover until he was certain that any open ground he had to cross was free from enemy observation. So it was coming dark again when at last he found himself only about half a mile from the fires of the Dog Warriors.

He left his horse there. He would have to go the rest of the way on his feet – or even on his stomach – if he were to

104

escape the observation of his quick-eyed enemies.

It took him at least two hours to traverse that next half-mile, and most of the way he went crouched as low as he could, and even at times, as he had guessed, crawling on his stomach. But at length he was past the sentries, who stood silent and watchful out among the trees away from the camp.

Perhaps those sentries weren't paying quite as much attention to their duties as they should have done; but then no eager young brave likes to stand on guard while the rest of his brothers celebrate a profitable victory with a Scalp Dance.

Redpath had heard of the Dog Soldiers' Scalp Dances, but this was the first time he had ever witnessed one. An enormous fire had been lighted in the open away from the lodges, and round it now was a great shuffling circle of warriors and maidens.

Drums were pounding and harsh Indian voices were lifted in wailing songs of victory. Those who had been successful in taking scalps that day had the grisly trophies of their success tied to their lances, which they held aloft as they danced.

The women always danced these Dog Warrior Scalp Dances, too. It was a dance that would probably last all night. Redpath thought it would kill most white men, but he knew that the athletic Dog Warriors would be on the war trail again with dawn.

It took him some time to spot the lodge in which the prisoners lay. Then he began to notice that as the boastful warriors danced past one certain tepee their shouts grew louder and more threatening, and they shook their lances at it. He guessed from that that the Indians were telling the prisoners within of the fate that was waiting for them.

It proved very difficult for the hunter to skirt round the circles of lodges and come up behind the one which contained the prisoners, but Redpath persevered, risking detection many times before he succeeded.

With his sharp knife he cut a way into the tepee. The firelight outside came through the open doorway, illuminating, though not very clearly, the interior. The noise from the triumphant warriors effectually drowned any noise that he made.

He peered in. Two huddled forms lay on the grass inside that bare lodge. They were wearing shirts and trousers and by that he knew them to be the men he was seeking. No one was on guard inside the tent with them, so he crawled carefully through the slit he had made in the buffalo hide and went across to them.

They weren't bound. Bonds weren't necessary to men in their condition. Plainly they had had further rough treatment upon their return to the Indians' camp. Betraying the secret of the arms cache apparently hadn't saved them from punishment at all.

They had been shockingly treated, and even the much-experienced hunter's face grew a little pale as he looked upon them.

Redpath pulled out his water-bottle and gave them a drink to revive them. Neither recognized him at first, but moaned as he lifted their heads. The scout kept whispering, 'It's me – Jim Redpath. Don't make any noise. Maybe I can help you.' Though even as he said it he knew it was impossible. These men were incapable of movement themselves, and manifestly it was beyond his powers to carry them away from the midst of these hostile Indians.

Riarn seemed not so far gone as Morg Day, and Redpath concentrated on him. 'What happened?' he asked. And when Riarn didn't answer, he tried to help him. 'You set off to bring in some more arms, didn't you?'

A faint 'Yes' issued from the bruised mouth.

'You ran into these Injuns an' they captured you?' Again that faint whisper – 'Yes.'

'Who was with you, and what happened to them?'

'Mick Culhedy and three 'breeds ... cousins of Joe Loup.'

'But not Joe Loup – or Stuart or Connor?'

He had to repeat the question before the near-dead man

answered him. 'No. They stayed . . . Sweet Water. Wish . . . I had. Reckon Joe knew it was dangerous.'

'Reckon he did,' said Redpath grimly. Outside a burst of frenzy from some nearby dancers startled him. A few excited warriors, not yet joined in the circle, rushed across to the prisoners' lodge and beat upon it with their clubs before racing away to find partners. Redpath froze into the shadows at the side of the doorway, his heart in his mouth, expecting them to enter and discover him. And when he saw what had happened to Riarn and Day he thought he would die before he'd let himself fall into their hands alive.

He had his Colt out as well as his Sharps repeater. The Colt would be useful if it came to close work, but the Sharps wasn't much good if anyone entered that lodge. He decided that five bullets from his Colt would find Indian billets; the sixth . . . would be turned against himself.

To his relief the danger passed, if only for the moment, anyway. It took all his courage to keep himself there, within that lodge with those two mangled human beings, but having come so far for information he wasn't prepared to depart without it.

Back he went to Riarn, who seemed to have fallen unconscious again. He bathed the bruised face as well as he could, and that brought Riarn to consciousness again, and then Redpath went on with his questioning.

'The Dog Men tortured you, an' you thought if you told about them guns you might be let free?'

'Sure – we should have known.' The reply crept painfully between the bruised and puffy lips. 'An' it did no good. They set on to us fer sport when they got us here. God, I wish I could die!' He started moaning quite loudly then, and it made something akin to panic come over the hunter. Then he decided that the moans would never be heard above the victory songs outside.

'Tell me, Riarn,' he whispered urgently, 'what happened to the ammunition? The Dog Soldiers got rifles only. Where'd you hide the ammunition?'

Riarn's whispered reply startled the hunter – the answer

was so obvious. 'We took it . . . that first trip cached the rifles because . . . boxes too heavy.'

'You took the ammunition – all of it – an' hid it in Sweet Water?' The faintest of nods from Riarn.

Behind them Morg Day began to whimper, and then they heard him start to moan, 'Keep 'em away! Don't let 'em touch me again! I can't stand any more; I can't stand any more!' Then his moans trailed off into a whimper that was like that of an ill-treated puppy. Redpath thought, 'That fellar hasn't long to live, whatever the Injuns decide to do to him.'

'Where's it hid?' he kept on.

' 'Breed place . . . Loup's relatives. But Joe was figgerin' on movin' it . . . Pawnees came an' frightened him.'

He seemed not to understand that this was the Jim Redpath who had come with those same Pawnees to Sweet Water.

The hunter rose slowly to his feet. Now that he had the information he knew that he must get away with it and seize hold of the hidden ammunition before it was sold to the Indians – perhaps to some Indians who would, in turn, trade it to the Dog Soldiers to fit their new rifles.

If he could destroy that ammunition or remove it it would temporarily anyway, neutralize any advantage those rifles gave to the Dog Soldiers.

Morg Day stirred again and begged, 'Kill me! Don't go an' leave us with these fiends!'

But that was something the scout could not do. Though it was an act of mercy, yet Redpath could not bring himself to kill these white men.

He stood over both men, talking quietly but insistently to them, while the leaping yellow firelight outside threw a great jumping shadow from his body on to the buffalo lodge wall behind him.

'Don't tell these Injuns about that ammunition. Don't let 'em know it's hid up in Sweet Water, else they'll go an' massacre every man, woman an' child in the settlement. You've given 'em guns – don't give 'em the ammunition to go with it!'

108

But for all he knew those tortured, tormented men never heard him. They lay in their bruises and blood, their jaws sagging with exhaustion, their eyes closed ... perhaps mercifully just then, finding peace from their sufferings in unconsciousness.

He had to leave them. He could do no good by staying, and with every minute that passed while he was in the lodge the chances of detection increased. Regretfully he left his renegades to their fate. Not even the thought that they had brought it upon themselves reduced the pity in his heart as he took a last farewell look at them. He knew how much they must yet endure before death pulled a final curtain across their sufferings.

He slipped out into the darkness behind the lodge. The Scalp Dance was still being noisily conducted around the great log fire; he felt pretty sure that interest in it would be so great that he stood a good chance of getting away unobserved. All the same, he never relaxed his vigilance and caution.

He was some distance away, possibly a couple of hundred yards among the tall grasses when he heard frightful screams that rose even higher than the chanting of the Scalp Dancers.

Redpath thought, 'I got away just in time!'

For some of the old men – too old, perhaps, to join in the warriors' dance, or perhaps cunning enough to feel that more could be wrought from the prisoners – must have returned to resume the torture of the prisoners.

Redpath increased his pace, frantic now to get away from the awful sound of tormented human beings. He could stand a lot of pain himself, and hardship and the sufferings of the open trail were common experience to him, to be borne with fortitude and without complaint. But that screaming ... That he could not stand.

He thought that perhaps in a desperate effort to buy death and so obtain release from their sufferings, the prisoners would shout out the secret of the scattered settlement at Sweet Water. If so, it would become a race between

Redpath and the Dog Men who reached the settlement first.

A lithe, strong form suddenly leapt on to him as he ran, stooped, into the tree belt. He had run bang into a Dog sentry!

The brave probably saw him just a second or so before he ran into the trees, and consequently his reaction was impulsive – he simply fell on top of the hunter and tried to brain him in the same movement with his tomahawk.

The only thing that saved Redpath was the rifle he was carrying stiffly extended from his body so as not to get it in his way. The brave didn't see the weapon and as he sprang up from the cover of the tall grasses he knocked into it and it threw him slightly off balance.

Immediately he felt his rifle knocked out of his hand, Redpath went flat and started to roll. He had a momentary consciousness of something heavy swinging just by his head – it was the tomahawk, and the blade smote on to a stone outcrop and broke away from the shaft.

The brave promptly dropped the useless piece of wood and grabbed viciously at the hunter's throat. Redpath fought like fury, knowing that if he lost this battle he would never fight another.

They rolled, flattening the dry grass and smashing into the brittle bushes – legs kicking, bodies heaving, hands gripping for vulnerable places. They made no noise other than the grunting from their exertions, they hadn't breath after the first impact for shouting or speaking.

Then it began to dawn on Redpath that he was losing this fight. Probably few white men could wrestle and defeat a Dog Soldier, for they were trained to a degree of fitness that was incredible even among redmen.

He put all his strength into an effort to break the grip around his throat that was squeezing the life out of him . . . and failed.

He was losing consciousness, weakening with every second. He fought to get breath into his lungs, but could not get it past the bruising thumbs that pressed his windpipe together.

So then he stopped trying to force those hands away. Instead he worked his right hand inside his shirt. His Colt was still there. He tried to drag it out, but could not, and now he was almost at his last gasp. So he pulled the trigger.

The explosion so close to his own body shook him, and burnt him. Nothing happened for quite a second after that, and then suddenly, all in one moment, that deadly grip went slack about his throat.

He heard the brave start to groan, as if badly hurt, but the hunter was so far gone that he could only lie there under his weight and not even attempt to throw him off.

The brave fell off without any effort from the hunter. He must have been shot through the stomach, and now he rolled away in agony, his knees doubling up to his chin, and his mouth opening to emit a frightful sound. He must have been in terrible pain.

Redpath got the breath back into his lungs and staggered to his feet. He felt that the Indians performing the Scalp Dance wouldn't have heard them because of the noise they were making, but he considered it more than likely that other sentries in this belt of trees would hear their comrade and come to investigate.

It took him seconds to find his new Sharps repeater, and all the while the Dog Man writhed and screamed his agony into the night air.

He found the rifle and started to run as fast as he could, deeper into cover. This was no time for caution; speed was essential, and he just had to hope that luck would be with him.

As he crashed through the bushes, Redpath heard other similar rushing sounds. Evidently assistance was coming up fast to the mortally wounded warrior.

Then a shouting arose – the harsh, guttural cries of the Cheyenne, from which tribe most of these Dog Men were descended. Almost at once Redpath realized that pursuit had been taken up – the Dog Warriors were on his track!

He slipped off his safety catch and gripped the Sharps ready for action. He had two considerable advantages – one that he knew where he was going and the Indians did not, and also there was the darkness to hamper the pursuit.

All the same, some fleet-footed warriors were very close to him by the time he found his horse and mounted. They were in a thicket less than thirty yards away, and when they heard the sound of hoofs they came running out, shouting their war cries and loosing off their arrows. Redpath was quick to notice that, for all their newly-acquired rifles, they used only arrows against him. It argued that the tribe did not have any reserves of suitable ammunition.

Once his horse jumped into its stride, Redpath did not fear pursuit. Mounted, he had too great an advantage over the Dog Men, fleet-footed though they were.

He rode south for a time, to throw possible pursuers off the track, then turned and headed west towards the Powder River.

The hunter came upon it much quicker than he had anticipated, and in fact rode out into the open along the edge of the river within a couple of hours. That made the presence of the Dog Soldiers very threatening to the scattered settlement of Sweet Water, for they could mount an attack in a matter of hours.

He dismounted and lay under cover until dawn, in order to find his bearings on the river. When daylight came he decided to ride downstream, and sure enough within a couple of miles he saw the first of the settlement buildings on the opposite bank.

When he came to the ferry he stood out prominently across the water from it, but though he waited half an hour the big flat pontoon did not come across to him. In time Redpath grew impatient, and remembering the Pawnee scout's report of a fordable place on the river a few miles downstream, he remounted and rode away to look for it.

Consequently, with one delay and another it was almost midday when he rode back into the settlement. He didn't appreciate the delay; it was essential that the settlement should have as great a warning as possible of the attack that he was certain was going to be launched upon it.

Not many people were about as he came riding in among the buildings, along the nearest thing to a street that the community possessed. He went straight up to the store, that being the most likely place to find men to whom he could deliver his warning. When he was within yards of it he realized two things.

One was that someone was shouting in great anger inside the store. The other – there were soldiers in the village.

Soldiers, and he was on the run from anything in uniform, he thought.

He drew rein outside the store. He had to give warning to the settlers before he started to think of his own safety—

Ann Churl came running out of the store, her face a little pale with fright. Then Judith walked out after her.

CHAPTER ELEVEN

SMOKE SIGNALS

Redpath had an impression of the sullen storekeeper standing within the place, shouting angry words after the girls – and the few men who were inside were little less vocal in their disapproval of them.

But he had eyes only for the girls. He saw Ann's eyes widen with horror as she saw him, saw her face go suddenly completely drained of all colour, then she took to her heels and ran as fast as her fashionable dress would permit her.

But Judith stood, ignoring the noise from the store behind her, and a smile of welcome had leapt into her face. He had no need to ask if she was pleased to see him – she was, and she wasn't bothered to disguise it. And he thought how much sweeter was the maid than the spoilt, pampered mistress—

Judith gestured behind her.

'They're not very friendly,' she said.

Redpath stooped in his saddle, placed his hands under her arms, and said 'Jump!'

As she jumped he lifted and swung her on to his horse before him.

'You're safe enough now,' he smiled.

Neither felt embarrassed; to neither came the thought that it was unusual for a man and a girl to be so close together upon such little acquaintance.

The hunter spurred away from the hostile men who were crowding into the doorway, though he had no particular aim in view. He asked, quickly, because he had a feeling that time was urgent: 'What are you doin' here, Judith? Why were those men shouting at you?' He had a glimpse of Ann in the distance, scurrying in most undignified manner towards a mounted cavalryman. Ann began to speak, pointed backwards, towards him.

Judith's firm, clear voice: 'The commissioner made a nuisance of himself because you escaped. He became too unpleasant, and so the fort commander ordered him to leave the fortress immediately, with all his party. The major made the excuse that he was expecting a big Indian attack shortly and would not be responsible for civilian lives within the fortress. But it was only an excuse – the army has no room for Indian Commissioners who want to supply Indians with arms.'

'No,' agreed Redpath. The distant cavalryman had gallantly dismounted and was walking away with Ann Churl, but every now and then he turned to look back at the hunter.

'We pulled into Sweet Water this morning. The major was so anxious to get rid of us that he gave us an escort of fifty cavalry to see us out of the district. We're taking this route because the other trail is deemed too unsafe at the moment.'

Redpath said grimly: 'Maybe it ain't any less safe than this way, Judith.' He was frowning, trying to decide what best to do and advise. 'I don't think the commissioner should venture out from the settlement for a while yet, not until we're sure there'll be no danger from the Dog Soldiers who're camped back there.' His wave indicated the far bank of the river.

'Stay here?' Judith's voice was comical in its dismay. 'Didn't you notice how well the commissioner's party is liked in Sweet Water?'

'You mean that row at the store?'

'Yes. We came along to buy some things. We never

115

expected trouble. But the moment we set foot in that dingy place an unpleasant fat man began to shout at us. There were three or four men in with him, and they weren't polite, either. I gather that these settlers, like Major Leabridge back at Fort Phil, don't care for people who come into the country to supply arms to Indians,' she ended with a smile.

Redpath said simply: 'Neither do I. Maybe within twenty-four hours you'll see what I mean.'

But Judith shook her head. 'I don't need convincing. I'm not like the obstinate, thick-headed commissioner!' She seemed very impatient with her self-satisfied employer. 'That raid upon our wagon train last week might have been a sham-Indian affair, but it was enough for me. I never want to see the real thing!' He felt her warm, strong young body shiver within his grip, and it seemed almost that she crept a little nearer to him.

He sighed. He would have been content to sit there holding her for ever, but he was here on a mission and it was vital that he accomplish it quickly. Far down the village he saw a group of cavalry gathering. His grip tightened on his rifle, for he knew what it meant. They were intending to ride down and recapture him again.

Reluctantly he lowered the girl to the ground. 'You'll be all right if you just keep walkin' towards your friends, the cavalry. I've got work to do. I came to warn the settlers that any moment now there'll be an attack upon them by the fiercest of all Indians – the Dog Soldiers.'

She looked up at him, her face concerned. She ignored the week-old beard on his chin, and saw only the man behind it – the kind of man she had never experienced back east before. Here was a bold and resolute frontiersman, yet one with a sense of responsibility or he would not have ridden in to give warning to the settlers when that meant risking his own skin. If there had been any lingering doubts before about him, they dissolved completely at that moment.

His face softened into a smile. 'I'll go back to the store to tell 'em, Judith. Looks like I'll be seein' you again, because I don't reckon I'll be able to leave this village for some time.'

He waved a parting salute and rode back to the store. The men were still standing in the doorway, sullen, angry, and unfriendly. The storekeeper called as he came up: 'Ef you're a friend of that blamed commissioner, you c'n keep outa here, fellar!'

Redpath dismounted without haste, deliberately tied up at the rail outside the store, then came and fronted the men.

'I know how you feel,' he told them. 'Guess I don't feel any better towards him myself.' He felt his audience drop some of their hostility at that. 'Maybe you might even be glad he decided to pay you a visit today,' he continued with a grim smile. 'He's brought fifty cavalry in with him, and I guess you're goin' to be glad of every gun before the day's out!'

'What do you mean?' A bearded settler shot out the question.

'Ever heard of the Dog Warriors?' The quick intake of breath showed they had. 'Wal, I guess right now they're on their way to pay Sweet Water a visit. I saw them doing a Scalp Dance last night, an' I'm darn certain you won't be long in seein' them.'

His words provoked consternation among his listeners. They looked quickly at each other, and exclaimed in dismay and horror – then looked back at the hunter as if seeking from him the lead that their chaotic thoughts couldn't work out for themselves. So Redpath put into words what they should have thought out but hadn't.

'Better drive all your stock into them corrals by the river. Better bring in everyone from the outlyin' parts. Go round an' warn everyone – an' get yourselves dug in so that the village can be defended agen the Dog Men when they come ridin' across the river.'

That reminded him.

'You'd better put a dozen men to cover the ford downstream.'

'A dozen?' Even now that storekeeper looked unpleasant and truculent, but Redpath was realizing that it was just his way and he meant nothing by his manner. 'Goldarn it, we won't have enough to defend the village ef you want a dozen men to watch the old ford!'

Redpath considered. 'Look, friend, you'n me had better go speak to this cavalry commander. Reckon he should get word back pronto to Fort Phil so they c'n send us reinforcements.'

'That'll take time.'

'We'll just have to fight 'em off an' buy time with lead an' powder,' was Redpath's prompt reply. 'An' for that we'll need the cavalry.'

The storekeeper stepped forward. 'I'm with you. Let's move.'

It was a signal for everyone to disperse. The other men all seemed galvanized into action in an instant. There was a great flurry of hoofs and legs swinging into creaking saddles, and then four horsemen went whipping their racing mounts down the trails that led to the outskirts of the settlement.

That left the hunter with the storekeeper. Redpath said: 'I'm Jim Redpath. I didn't tell you when I was here last.'

'Redpath?' the storekeeper said. His sour face wrinkled in thought. 'I think I've heard of you. I'm Mike Grew.'

They were walking together. Redpath leading his mount. Approaching were five cavalrymen. One seemed to be an officer; as they came nearer the hunter saw it was a young lieutenant.

So he said to the storekeeper: 'Mike, I want to tell you something. These fellars will try to take me prisoner as soon as they come up to me.'

Mike Grew halted and looked at him, his little eyes blinking in the bright sunlight. 'What you done wrong?' he asked.

'A girl said I tried to assault her.' Grew looked hard at him at that. 'I didn't.' Redpath shrugged. 'But you don't have to believe me. They were goin' to tie me to a cart wheel an' give me fifty lashes – that was back at Fort Phil. But I escaped, an' I don't intend to be taken back simply because I came to warn Sweet Water of a Dog Soldiers' attack.'

Mike considered, his manner apparently one of unrelieved distaste. 'Yeah, that wouldn't be fair,' he said at length. 'A fellar shouldn't be flogged because he came to help folks like us.' He looked at the bulge under Redpath's shirt. 'I don't carry a gun. That looks like a Colt in there. Maybe ef you let me have it I could help you stand up to them soldiers.'

Redpath hesitated. To give that Colt was to reduce his own effectiveness if it came to a close-quarters' struggle – and if Mike Grew wasn't on the revel and turned the gun against him. . . .

Mike said impatiently, almost nastily 'Give me that gun, Redpath. I won't go agen you.' And somehow it was convincing. Redpath withdrew it and handed it across.

Then the cavalry came up, and the four young cavalrymen tried to surround the pair. Redpath was ready for it and stepped to one side so that he had his back to a split-paling fence. His gun was half up, ready.

The lieutenant was very young and shouldn't have been so far away from his mother, the hunter thought ironically. But he was bred in the tradition of the cavalry and was cool and brave besides.

He spurred forward until he could look down at Redpath, and then he said quite calmly: 'You're Redpath, aren't you? I suppose you want to give yourself up?'

Redpath jerked up the muzzle end of his gun, his eyes watching those men around him. Mike Grew was standing between two of them, facing him and he still had lingering doubts about the sourfaced storekeeper.

'Does this look as if I want to give myself up?'

'If you don't, I'll take you by force,' the lieutenant said confidently.

Redpath snapped back the safety catch. 'Try it,' he encouraged. The men didn't, and the officer was prudent enough not to order them forward.

Instead he said, still as confident as ever: 'You won't get away with this, Redpath. I'll see you never get out of this settlement.'

'Maybe I'll have something to say about that,' was the hunter's dry rejoinder. 'I won't stand for bein' flogged for something I never did.' Then his voice changed; it became brisk and impersonal, almost curt.

'Just forget about me for the moment, lootenant. I came to Sweet Water today because I've a strong hunch that four hundred Dog Warriors – maybe more – will attack the settlement before long. I rode in to give warnin'.'

The lieutenant smiled. 'It will be nice meeting them,' he said cheerfully.

Mike Grew stepped forward at that, his face more hang-dog and sullen than ever. They didn't know, as Redpath now knew, that it was just his manner, and the hunter saw the lieutenant stiffen, as if anticipating an attack.

But Mike just growled. 'That's all right for you army men, but what about the women an' children in this settle-ment? Me, I think it'd be nice ef we never saw another Injun.'

'Look, time's passin',' Redpath interposed quickly. 'The settlers are bein' brought in right now, but they'll never be able to hold a scattered settlement like this, not with only around a hundred people with guns.'

'We won't have as many as that, Jim,' Mike Grew said sourly.

'Then that's all the more reason why you should stay on in Sweet Water. lootenant. You an' your men are needed here, not on the trail guardin' that fat-bellied commis-sioner.'

The lieutenant smiled. 'That's for the commissioner to decide,' he said.

'Then,' said the hunter acidly, 'when you see him tell him that he is the cause of any danger now threatening Sweet Water.'

He felt Mike Grew's eyes come round to him. He hadn't

intended to let this news out in the village, but he felt that circumstances now demanded it to be known.

'The commissioner brought rifles and ammunition into the territory.' They all knew that, of course, but not what followed. 'The Dog Warriors tortured the secret of the rifles out of a couple of renegades, an' almost the last thing I heard as I left the Dog Men's camp last night were the screams of those two men as the rest of the secret was bein' torn from 'em '

'What d'you mean, Jim?' Mike Grew asked quickly.

'All the ammunition – fifty thousand rounds – on the commissioner's train, was brought to Sweet Water an' hidden here. Those rifles aren't much good to the Dog Men without ammunition, an' my guess is they'll attack Sweet Water just to get it.'

Mike Grew gasped. 'That commissioner fellar's a lot to answer for! Ef he tries to leave us—'

The lieutenant laughed. 'You don't think I'm fool enough to swallow that yarn, do you, Redpath?' He looked across at the storekeeper. 'Don't you see, this fellow is lying – he's walked into a trap – he didn't know we were in the village, and this is an attempt to dodge us again.' Suddenly his hand went to the revolver in the holster on his belt.

'Come on, you. Put down that gun or I'll give my men orders to shoot you down!'

Mike Grew pulled out his Colt and stuck it against the lieutenant's side. 'It wouldn't be healthy fer you ef you did,' he said sombrely.

The army officer's eyes narrowed, but the smile never left his boyish face. 'You're asking for trouble, too, fellow. But I'll give you a chance. Why do you believe this outlaw in preference to a United States officer?'

Grew's face went sourer and sourer as he heard the youthful arrogance. Then he said contemptuously: 'Because I never saw the army get anythin' right. I've got a hunch you're wrong in Redpath's case, too.'

The lieutenant nodded as if not worried by the insult. 'I'll remember that fellow later,' he called, then he gave an

121

order to his men and they all rode back through the settlement.

Redpath breathed his relief. 'Mike,' he told him, 'you were a great help. That's somethin' I won't forget in a hurry.'

'Ef the Injuns attack, we'll all be in your debt fer gettin' through with a warning,' was all that the big storekeeper said in reply.

He handed the Colt back to Redpath, saying that he had one just as good back in his store, then he turned to find out what was happening about defence preparations. Redpath began to realize that the storekeeper was a man of importance around the settlement.

Already the place was getting busier as some men came galloping in from the fields, and a woman with two children was hurrying across a path from an isolated wickiup. But for the moment Redpath couldn't figure out what part he could play in the defence programme.

Suddenly he remembered a man with a lump of flesh between his eyes, a furtive retiring creature. He walked back, still leading his horse, and approached the ferryman's wickiup. He thumped a few times on the door, but no one opened it.

He was turning away when a voice that was surprisingly high-pitched asked: 'You want the ferryman, mister?' It was that toothless old man of the other day.

'Yes,' Redpath said. 'You know where he is?'

'Me? No, I don't. I ain't seen him since a coupla days ago. Folks around here got kinda nasty about him helpin' some renegades get rifles fer trade with them blamed Redskins. He skipped off in the night. Guess he kinda figured it mightn't be healthy for him around here ef he stayed.'

His eyes watered suddenly, then his trembling hand came out with an old, old corn cob.

'Mister, I don't get much baccy. Now you wouldn't be wantin' ter give me any fer that information, would you?'

Redpath nodded, thinking. 'I might do at that.' He

pulled out his tobacco and gave some leaf to the old fellow. 'Maybe I'd give you some more if you thought real hard,' he said.

The old man cackled. 'Me, I'm thinkin' already,' he quavered.

Patiently he began to question the man. Had he seen any men around the village who had maybe a dozen or more packhorses? Men who were thick with the ferryman and brought their horses over the river after dark? No-good, low, no-account fellars, they'd be, he supplemented.

It didn't get him far. Apparently, according to the old man, the village was full of no-good, no-account fellars. And he didn't remember anyone using the ferry ever at nights to bring horses across. In explanation it came out that he spent most nights at the primitive bar in the store, and consequently he couldn't be expected to see any ferrying operations.

Redpath nearly gave in then, especially when it became obvious that so far as the village was concerned, Joe Loup was unknown, as were the other white renegades, of whom only Stuart and Jep Connor were now alive.

He rose to go, then an idea occurred to him. 'That gal who lived in his hut – she was his daughter?'

The old man's eyes fixed greedily upon the tobacco in the hunter's hand. 'Yep, that gal shore was.'

'Her mother was an Injun?'

'A 'breed. Lives out beyond the willow belt.'

Redpath felt that he was getting somewhere at last. Tantalizingly he held out half his tobacco stock. 'Tell me about that family.'

The old man spat. 'They're lower'n low,' he gabbled. 'They ain't liked none at all round here. Reckon they're just a thievin' bunch of no-goods that's no better'n redskins.'

'How many are in the family?'

'There's the old woman – a squaw woman. Her husband's dead, got killed in a ruckus over some cattle stealin'. An' the boys, her sons, are the very devil.' Again he

123

spat his disgust. 'There's around six or eight of 'em; I don't know fer sure. 'Breeds – quick with their tempers, an' always in trouble. They keep well to themselves.'

'Would they have pack horses or mules – maybe as many as a dozen?'

'They got some hosses around their place, but I don't know about havin' a dozen. A dozen's a mighty lot to own in these parts. Reckon, though, they'd be capable of findin' hosses in plenty ef they figgered it was worth their while.'

Redpath rose, satisfied. He felt tolerably certain by now that these would be some of Joe Loup's relatives – they would be the Indian raiders on the commissioner's wagon train that day, and probably somewhere in the vicinity of the 'breeds' smallholding the lot would be buried.

He mounted. That ammunition would be useful if it came to a siege of the village. The old man gave detailed instructions about a willow patch beyond which the 'breeds' place lay, and Redpath spurred away quickly. He wanted to find that ammunition if at all possible before action started around the village.

As he rode inland to where a line of willows grew alongside a tributary of the Powder River, he heard galloping in the near-distance. He turned in his saddle. Ten men were riding down-river as hard as they could go. He guessed they would be the party sent out, as he had suggested, to hold the ford below the settlement. He knew it wouldn't stop the ferocious Dog Warriors from crossing – they would swim their horses over if they found the ford was held – but it would at least delay them in their attack.

He looked across the river, and the muscles of his jaw suddenly tightened.

Not far back across the Powder River smoke was rising in the air. He was no expert on smoke signals, but this particular one he knew.

It was a call to war.

CHAPTER TWELVE

TOO LATE!

He had seen that same signal used before, down near Fort Laramie. It was the Cheyenne signal, but then the Dog Men were originally Cheyenne tribesmen, so that wasn't remarkable.

He guessed that the call to war could only mean an attack on Sweet Water, but there was another inference to be derived from it.

It meant that there were other Dog Warriors in the territory and they were being called up to join in the fighting – either that or the Dog Men were enlisting the aid of some tribe other than their own.

Whichever way it was, it meant that the attack on Sweet Water, when it came, would be mounted by considerably more than the estimated four hundred warriors that was his original calculation.

For a few seconds he sat and looked at that signal, thin and black and curling into the blue autumn sky. Then his doubts were resolved for him.

A girl came hurrying along the path before him. With her were two small, ragged children and a squaw woman of advanced years.

The girl was wearing a bonnet that was gay with ribbons.

Redpath spurred up to her. When she saw who it was she became frightened and spoke quickly to the wrinkled squaw woman. Redpath stopped them.

The girl cried in terror. 'We didn't do no harm, mister. There's Injuns comin' – a big attack; a fellar just rode in and told us. We want to get among the huts.'

'Where's your father? And the boys from back yonder?' Redpath demanded sternly – nodding towards the willow belt.

'They've gone.' She spoke quickly, desperate to be on her way into the settlement now. Her words had the smack of truth about them, for all her shifty manner of speaking.

'When did they go? An' where?'

'They lit out after that fellar came ridin' in. He told 'em you was back in the village, an' Joe—'

'Joe Loup?' he asked quickly.

'Yeah, Joe Loup,' the girl said. 'He's my man. You won't hurt him, mister, will you?'

'Depends on Joe,' he told her shortly. 'What happened to him – an' Connor an' Stuart? An' the 'breeds?'

'They rid off till the shootin' died. Don't know where they aimed ter go – they jes' went off. Now let us go, mister. It's the truth I'm tellin' you.'

Redpath asked one more question. 'Did they take any lead hosses with 'em?' If they did it meant they had got away with that ammunition, so precious to any Indians in the territory.

She shook her head. 'They jes' rid off, I tell you – fast.'

That meant, then, that the ammunition would still be in its cache somewhere around the willow belt! Reluctantly he let the frightened little party scurry on. It wasn't fair to hold them out here when any time Indians might come storming up to the settlement, killing everyone within sight as they did so.

He wanted to ask questions about the loot – probably the girl wouldn't know where it was hidden, but he felt sure the old squaw woman would have more than an idea.

'They won't get away from Sweet Water,' he told himself. 'I'll start askin' questions later, when I see how much time I have on my hands.' If the 'breeds and the renegades had bolted, there was no apparent vital hurry to discover the cache. But that smoke signal did demand urgent attention.

He pulled round and sent his horse thundering round the wickiups of smallholders, the flying hoofs kicking up clouds of dust from the dry, grey-black soil. It took him only a few minutes to get back among the more solid buildings around the store – probably the original buildings of the settlement. When he reached them he saw a sight that startled him.

One solitary covered wagon stood in a sea of angry people. Up beside the teamster he saw the red and angry face of the portly commissioner, while just behind, revealed by the tied-back cover, were Ann and her mother – and Judith.

Holding back the crowd of irate settlers was the young lieutenant and his cavalry; but it wasn't pleasant work because there were women in that crowd and they were made desperate by fear and were even more threatening in their attitude than their menfolk.

Redpath called down to a bearded, soiled and tattered settler on the outskirts of the crowd. 'What's bitin' everyone?' But above the din his own shout came as a whisper.

He saw that bearded mouth open and caught the reply only by bending low out of his saddle.

'It's that danged commissioner. He won't stop an' help with the defence of Sweet Water. No, sir, he's in too big a hurry to get to a telegraph to report the army fer not playin' wet nurse to him, I reckon.'

'He's on his way out?' Redpath sat back in his saddle. That was bad news. It mean they would be short of fifty good fighters – worse, that Judith was to be exposed once again to the perils of the trail by that Eastern talking-box.

The thought sent him into the crowd. They gave way before his horse, though many wondered what part he had in this affair. When he came out into the clear space around the ring of cavalry, he lifted his hands for silence. It came, though it was slow in coming, because those settlers were fighting mad and hated to be baulked of their prey like this.

The lieutenant came cantering up. Redpath had to admire the youngster. He hadn't turned a hair in spite of the threatening situation in which he found himself. They looked over their horses' heads at each other.

'Are you wrong in your head, tryin to make the trail out?' Redpath called. 'Haven't I warned you, there's Injuns in the territory – hostile Dog Men?'

The lieutenant replied coolly: 'The commissioner wants to move out.' There was a savage shout from the pressing, wildly angry mob. 'We don't blame him!'

When it died away, the lieutenant said calmly: 'I don't care what lies ahead. I've been put at the disposal of the commissioner, to obey any orders he gives. If he says take the trail, I take it.' Then his young voice became hard. 'And if anyone attempts to interfere with those orders—'

'Well?'

'I'll shoot my way out.'

One look at that determined young face and Redpath knew he meant it.

He turned to the crowd. 'You'll have to wait for your vengeance on the commissioner,' he called. 'Let him go through—' An angry roar of disapproval from the crowd. 'You can't afford to lose valuable men fighting these soldiers,' he shouted. 'Heck! Let them through and get to your posts! There's a smoke signal back there – it's Cheyenne, an' it's callin' for war. I'll say it means war against Sweet Water! Let 'em through, I tell you!'

He rode into the crowd and they fell back reluctantly. The lieutenant rode after him, and behind came the cavalry with that solitary wagon in their midst. When the move was started, Redpath pulled into the crowd and stood there until the wagon was abreast of him. He saw Judith craning to look across at him. He saw that her face was pale and filled with uncertainty, and her left hand plucked nervously at the neck of her dress.

'Judith,' he called. 'Don't go with that blamed pighead of a commissioner. He'll never get through alive. Stay here with me – I'll look after you!'

A curious silence descended on the crowd then, so that everyone heard what followed.

The commissioner looked round in surprise. Judith didn't move for a couple of seconds, then suddenly she started to clamber over the tail of the wagon. A cheer went up from some of the settlers. Perhaps the romance that is in all people was touched by the incident – or perhaps they felt that in some way they were scoring a victory over the commissioner.

Henry Churl spoke to the driver, who promptly pulled up. He shouted back to Judith: 'If you get off here, I wash my hands of you. You'll not only be an ingrate, but also a fool. Only a fool would entrust herself to a man who has so recently faced a charge as serious as that lodged against that blackguard!'

In his passion he pointed his finger at Redpath, but the effect was rather marred because it was fat and trembled with the rage that consumed him at that moment.

Henry Churl was a very bitter man. He had come west feeling sure that his name would go down to posterity as the man who made peace with the Indians. Instead of which he found himself being sent ignominiously home, his mission worse than a failure, and he the butt of all the ill-temper and rudeness of these settlers on his route. He had had enough, and now he found that his vexation seemed principally directed against the man whom he thought had tried to assault his daughter.

Now, he thought furiously, no matter the consequences, he would not stay here in Sweet Water, simply because that seemed to be the wish of the man he hated!

And his fury reached – and passed – boiling point when Judith started to move towards the wagon's tail.

Redpath saw the girl pause, as if to let the commissioner's words sink in, as if to reflect on what he said. Then she lifted her eyes and looked across again at Redpath. He didn't say anything more; the decision was up to the girl now.

She seemed to nod, as if her mind was made up. Then she called: 'Help me down, Jim. I'm coming with you!'

129

Incautiously the hunter spurred in among the cavalrymen. The commissioner was nearly falling off his high
perch as he strove to look back at them. Just before
Redpath pulled round to help the girl out, Henry Churl
shouted: 'What sort of a girl are you, to go with a man who
tried to assault your mistress?'

Judith held out her arms and Redpath took her and put
her gently before him. He pulled a couple of yards away
from the wagon, so that they could see the purpling face
of the portly commissioner. It was the girl who spoke,
though Redpath was trying to get his tongue round the
words.

'I don't believe he ever touched her,' she called. 'She's
vindictive enough for anything, your daughter!'

It gave Redpath courage, a courage he had never
possessed before, to defend himself against that awful
charge. But then he was being viciously slandered in front
of people who might be his neighbours in time to come.

He spoke up to the commissioner. 'Look your daughter
in the eye, and ask her – "Did Redpath save you from the
Indians that day, and did you reward him by lying because
he would not make love to you?" Ask her that, and see what
you think, commissioner!'

'I won't stand to have my daughter insulted by a blackguard like you, Redpath!' Henry Churl shouted. And he
pulled a derringer unexpectedly out of his sleeve.

A roar of fury rose from the crowd. Their sympathies
were with the big, rough-looking hunter; he looked their
own kind. And they hated the fat commissioner, anyway.
They came surging forward again, arms waving, fists threatening, over a hundred irate, incensed pioneers and their
wives.

The lieutenant saw the danger. He came spurring back
and put himself between the derringer and Redpath.
More and more the hunter had to admire the guts of the
kid.

'Put that gun away, or I won't be responsible for your
safety,' rapped the officer, and his tone was so commanding

that in spite of his temper, Churl slipped that gun back up his sleeve.

'Now start rolling,' the lieutenant ordered, and the driver flourished his whip and sent it cracking over the backs of his team of four horses – only four because they were travelling light.

They moved. Someone shouted 'You're a danged passel o' fools! You'll never get through alive. You c'n go without me!' And when Redpath looked there was old Lem standing alongside his horse – Lem and the other fellow called Luke, who had come in with the wagon train.

Redpath shouted above the hubbub. 'I've got a lot to thank you for, Lem. I'll do it if we come out of this alive.'

Then the swirling crowd parted them, and he never saw the old-timer alive after that.

The wagon and its cavalcade of troopers went quickly down the river trail; the settlers sorted themselves out and began to take orders from one or two of their number, one being the fat, sour-looking storekeeper.

In a moment they found themselves sitting alone on top of the horse. Redpath smiled at the girl, and she smiled back at him. He said: 'You're takin' less of a risk by stayin' here than if you went on that trail, I think.'

'I'd have stayed, even though the risk was greater.'

He studied her reply, then asked weakly: 'Why?'

She laughed openly in his face. 'Oh, Jim, you're not as clever as I thought you were! Just put me down and work it out!'

In a kind of stupor he lowered her gently to the ground.

'Where are you goin'? What are you goin' to do, Judith?' he demanded, but his thoughts were still on the implications of that last little speech of hers. He was coming to the conclusion that it could mean only one thing. . . .

Judith looked across at the store. A lot of women were working there, helping the men to open up cases of ammunition. 'I guess I'll give a hand there, Jim,' she told him, and started across.

As he watched her hurry away from him, with all those

people closing round her as if to imprison her within their midst, an agony of doubt came into his mind. He wanted to believe, yet couldn't quite, didn't dare. But he felt he couldn't go away without knowing one way or another.

He shouted – because he had to shout over that babel of sound – 'Judith, what did you mean? Don't go without tellin' me.'

He saw her pause among the crowd; she was tall enough to stand out among the settler women. She looked across at him and laughed. It gave him courage.

'Do you mean you'd – marry me?' he shouted.

Every woman there stopped talking on an instant; every woman turned to look at the girl standing in their midst. It was disconcerting to the hunter, upon his horse, but it didn't seem to embarrass the girl a bit.

'I thought you meant that when I was on the commissioner's wagon,' she called. 'That's why I got off!'

At which every settler woman expanded into a great smile of relief, happy in the thought of the romance that had blossomed right before their sentimental if weather-beaten noses. And Redpath rode away with his heart singing.

Redpath rode quickly across to where the storekeeper was issuing some new guns, and at that moment he felt a match for all the Dog Men in America! Mike looked up, that perpetual expression of annoyance and distaste on his face, but Redpath seemed to see behind it a twinkle of pleasure, as if the hunter found favour in Mike Grew's sight. 'Mike, how 'bout sendin' someone off to Fort Phil to get help?'

Mike considered. 'Maybe we should wait a while, Jim. So far we ain't seen a blamed redskin. We'll fix fer a couple of boys to be ready to ride the moment an attack develops, huh?'

'I leave it to you.' He pulled his horse's head round. 'I'll just ride round a while to see what's goin' on.'

A lot of people were streaming in towards the vicinity of the store. Some rode up with wagons piled with their belongings, while others came afoot but carrying bundles on their shoulders. A camp was being set up within the buildings of the settlement to house the women and children until after the fighting.

Redpath rode out against a stream of lowing cattle, reluctant mules and plodding horses; there were goats and sheep and even geese being driven in by barefooted boys. The children seemed to think it was all grand fun, but the parents looked harassed and weary. They knew the meaning of Indian warfare – knew it too well.

About twenty minutes later the first shot was fired in the battle of Sweet Water. Redpath was riding back into the crowded settlement, through the lines of armed settlers who had dug trenches between the strongest-built huts, and were manning the log cabins themselves.

A solitary rifle-shot crackled in the distance, downstream. Everyone stopped talking and working at that; everyone listened for more, and then their eyes sought each other's and there was dread in them.

If there had been any doubts before about an impending Indian attack, then now they had none. And because the attackers would be Dog Warriors, they knew it would be a bitter battle, with all their lives at stake.

A few seconds later a ragged fusillade of fire broke out, and after that the firing became constant though intermittent in intensity. Five minutes later a messenger came racing in from the ford. He pulled up in the open space before Mike Grew's and shouted out his message for all to hear:

'They tried ter cross the ford – Dog Men, hundreds of 'em! We let 'em get started, then we opened up an' killed a lot. But they've gone ridin' right downstream, an' we can't leave the ford to go after 'em. They're goin' ter swim across.'

Mike shouted to a couple of fifteen-year-olds waiting eagerly by a pair of fine, strapping horses, 'Git goin', boys! Make Fort Phil Kearney or bust! They've got to send some of them useless soldiers down to help us!'

133

The boys swarmed into their saddles like a couple of excited monkeys, and spurred away on their dangerous mission without further ado. Then Mike called across to the mounted Redpath, 'Hey, there, scout, you go down an' see what's happenin' below the ford.'

Redpath lifted his hand in salute and pulled away. Judith saw him over the heads of the crowd and he heard her call, 'Take care, Jim!'

He waved to her, then rode off, followed by the messenger.

Before he reached the ford he began to see Indians on the opposite bank. There were a lot of them, but they weren't doing anything particularly formidable. Redpath guessed that their part in the battle was to keep the defenders at the ford while their fellow braves swam the river at a lower place.

At this point the river took a wide bend, so Redpath left the trail and rode into the low hills in order to see what was happening a few miles downstream. Ten minutes later he came out on to the river again – it had been rough going, but he must have saved a couple of miles by it.

He found that he was too late. Already a sizeable force of Dog Men was standing on the west bank, within a quarter of a mile of him.

And just at that moment he saw the slow-moving commissioner's wagon come riding into view around a bend in the river road, the cavalry trotting in two groups before and after it.

CHAPTER THIRTEEN

THE ATTACK!

About two dozen braves were across, but a long line of horsemen were swimming their mounts in towards the west bank, so that every moment the number grew larger. When they saw the wagon and its cavalcade of cavalry, the Dog Warriors, without the slightest hesitation, rode up the trail to launch an attack. These Dog Men fought with seeming disregard to odds.

Almost immediately, though, Redpath realized there was a plan behind the bold approach. The idea was to delay the cavalry until further reinforcements crossed the river and the Dog Men would thus be able to launch an overwhelming assault upon the soldiers.

Redpath could do nothing to help them. If anything he had a feeling almost of pleasure that, whether he wanted it or not, the commissioner was now having to help the settlers by occupying, at least for some time, the attentions of the savage enemy. Then the pleasure left him as he remembered the two women in that wagon. He thought, 'Thank God, Judith didn't go with them!'

He saw the cavalry charge suddenly. That boyish lieutenant was a pretty discerning young man – he must have seen through the Dog Men's tactics and was now trying to fight his way through them, anticipating that, once through, the Indians would leave them to go their way while they resumed their attack on the settlement.

His plan would no doubt have succeeded but for the fact that the wagon, with only four horses, could not by any means keep pace with his cavalry. The result of it was that he had to stop his men and bring them back around the wagon, otherwise cunning Indians would have come circling in behind his leading troops.

All at once it seemed that the west bank became alive with the enemy. A great batch of Indian horsemen arrived all at the same moment and came urging their dripping steeds out of the water to join in the fight.

The lieutenant must have realized that now he had no chance of fighting his way through, and instead he turned his troops and the wagon off from the trail and came racing in towards the foothills where Redpath was standing. It took the hunter a few seconds to realize that in fact the cavalcade was following a minor trail that paralleled a willow-lined tributary of the Powder River.

He took a swift glance round to get his bearings, then decided that this was the same tributary upon whose east bank the 'breeds had their smallholding – this would be the trail they used when they wanted to join the river road.

Clearly the lieutenant realized that on the open trail by the river's edge the eager Dog Soldiers would surround them and quickly cut them to pieces, but in the low, rolling hills away from the river there was a chance to make a stand.

Redpath was some distance away, and unable to assist the cavalry, even if he had wanted to. He sat his mount and watched the race. At first the cavalry held off the galloping Indians with some good shooting from their saddles, but when all their guns were empty and the going was too rough to give them a chance to reload, the Dog Warriors came racing ahead and around and forced them to stop.

The courageous young lieutenant immediately caused his men to dismount all around a steep little knoll which gave cover, and prepared to fight it out.

Redpath saw the siege begin, then his attention was

diverted to the main river again. Now the Indians were coming across in hundreds, and he began to see that with the Dog Warriors were men of other tribes, mostly Cheyenne but probably Dakotas, too. There was no doubt now that the Indians were massed to meet the threat of a new military road through their hunting grounds, and were intent on first getting that hidden ammunition as a prelude to striking back at Colonel Endricks' force.

By the water's edge Redpath saw a conference of chiefs of several tribes. Evidently they were debating strategy now they had successfully accomplished the crossing of the river barrier. In a few moments that strategy became apparent to the watching hunter.

A large force was left to besiege the commissioner's wagon and its bodyguard. The main bulk of warriors, however, went racing away along the river trail towards the settlement, intent on destroying it without further loss of time.

Redpath didn't want to get cut off, and he started round to gallop back to the settlement. He had actually started to retrace his steps when his eye was caught by a movement from a small band of mounted braves who were proceeding at right-angles to the main mass on the river road.

He at once drew rein again to see what this manoeuvre betokened.

There were about fifty warriors in this party, all Dog Men in war bonnets and war paint. They were riding in single file, probably following a path along the bank of the willow-lined tributary.

Suddenly an exclamation escaped the sharp-eyed hunter. Well up with the leaders of this party was a double-laden horse. One of the riders was an Indian: but the man being supported in front of the painted brave was – Rupe Riarn!

At once Redpath understood. Riarn had been kept alive so that he could lead the Indians to the hiding-place of the so highly prized ammunition.

The army scout put his heels into his horse's sides, and

that surprised animal shot away over the hills as if a gun had been exploded in its ear. As he rode furiously back towards the settlement, Redpath heard a steady crackle of rifle-fire from the besieged cavalry on that abrupt little knoll between him and the river.

Then, approaching the settlement, he heard heavy firing from up-river.

It startled him. The braves from downstream, coming by the circuitous river trail, could not have reached the settlement ahead of him. He could only think that another Indian force must have swum the river from a point upstream of Sweet Water and was attacking the settlement from the south.

Much smoke was now rising in the distance, as if buildings were on fire in the outlying parts of the settlement. As he came up among the nearest wickiups he saw one take fire and go up in flames. Galloping away were a couple of settlers. Evidently they were destroying their own remote homes rather than leave them standing to provide cover for the approaching Indian masses.

Redpath galloped between two fortified log cabins. The defenders shouted for news from him, but he hadn't time to answer. Racing between the closer-set buildings, he rode out before the store, that meeting place for all activity.

A defence committee seemed by now to have been set up and was giving orders. Redpath rode across to it. Now the firing from the south was sustained and heavy, and the smoke from many a burning wickiup kept drifting in on the centre of the settlement where the leaders of the defenders were gathered.

A bearded old patriarch shouted, 'What news, brother?'

Panting, Redpath delivered it, as quickly as possible.

'The commissioner an' the cavalry are surrounded an' cut off. Two or three hundred Injuns are ridin' in to attack from downstream. But a party's set off to get that ammunition. They seem to know where it is. If they get that ammunition, with them Henry rifles they'll wipe this settlement out in no time!'

The patriarch began: 'We haven't any men to spare.'

Redpath said curtly, 'Then you'd better find some! You won't have any men at all if they get hold of those cartridges!'

He felt sorry for the harassed old man, even so. It was true there weren't any men to spare – yet equally true that men must be found to keep the Indians back from the 'breeds' holding.

'All right.' The grey-bearded old settler made up his mind. 'Do what you can with five men, will you?'

Five! It startled Redpath. Only five – six with himself – to combat the fifty-strong party of Dog Men! Then he recognized that he could expect no more, so he nodded. He thought, 'My Sharps is worth a dozen men, anyway!'

Five men were hastily summoned. One was a cripple with a twisted leg, two were but kids. That was the kind of force they had to use in the defence of Sweet Water.

They thundered out, back among the outlying defence posts. Redpath's idea was to get to the 'breeds' place ahead of the slower-moving Indians, trotting along that winding path by the tributary, and defend it as long as they could. He knew it was pretty hopeless, because the place itself was probably a pretty hopeless place to defend. But whatever time they gained was to the advantage of the people back in the settlement – they had to buy time for the men, women and children there, even if the price was their lives.

As they swept over a small hill, just about the place where Redpath had met the 'breed girl before, a groan came through his lips.

They hadn't raced fast enough!

The Indians were already in sight along the path by the tributary. If Redpath and his party attempted to make a run for the cover of the farm buildings, for certain the Indians would cut across and hack them down before they reached it.

Redpath thought, 'There's only one thing for it!' He gave the order to dismount. Their only chance of keeping the Indians back from the buildings within which he was sure the stolen ammunition lay, was to shoot down any who attempted to cross the open space around the farm. In time the Indians were sure to creep up under cover of the tributary banks and gain the place, but at least they would have to do it afoot, and that was a lot slower than riding through on horseback.

The Indians had seen them and were halted, trying to appraise the situation. Several of them appeared to carry guns, but Redpath thought they would be old muzzle-loaders, captured in the wars with the army. They weren't formidable, compared with the swifter-loading Henrys with which his party was armed, though of course their range was infinitely greater than the more usual Indian weapon, the bow and arrow.

The hunter led them at a run to a point overlooking the tumbling, dilapidated farm buildings – a typical 'breed place. Here an outcrop of rock provided a lot of good, natural shelter, and a long, rather steep slope down to the farm was clear of cover, so that any attackers would suffer heavily in attempting to storm their defence. Only a few yards to their right was a trail – a poor one, apparently little used. Redpath guessed that this was the same trail along which the lieutenant had turned his party, and by the side of which even now he was standing siege.

Throwing himself down behind some rocks, he listened for a moment. There was some firing from back over the hill, and Redpath thought it would be from the besieged cavalry. It wasn't very heavy, and that was a good omen to the scout. It suggested that without great effort the strongly armed soldiers were standing off the Indian attack.

One of the kids with him shook his arm. 'I saw somebody. There's somebody down among the buildings!'

But no one else had seen anything, and they decided that the kid was mistaken. Probably it was one of the horses moving around in search of grass back along the water's edge, Redpath thought. He was surprised to see so many horses left at the farm. Usually when people left their homesteads they took care to take any spare horses with them.

The Indians at that moment decided to try to gallop across to the buildings among the willows. Screaming their war cries, they bent low over their horses' streaming manes and flogged them into their best efforts.

Redpath shouted, 'Aim for the hosses!' That was always the most effective way of stopping a charge. A volley rang out, and six horses either crashed headlong or went staggering in agony out of the race. At that range it wasn't hard to hit a horse, even though it was going at full gallop.

Redpath kept pumping shells into his Sharps while his companions reloaded. His Sharps was a magnificent weapon, and by now most Indians knew of the newly invented repeater and hated to come across it in their wars. Only the stupidity of the War Department back in Washington prevented a proportion of every troop and corps from being issued with the dreaded repeaters.

He didn't count his score, but he guessed that every bullet found a target in that massed horseflesh. Then he reloaded, while his companions took up the fire.

That unexpectedly fierce burst of firing unnerved the Indians and turned them from their target. Suddenly they went swerving away, those who still remained mounted, and rode down a gully that branched off from the tributary. Occasionally Redpath could see feathered war bonnets, but when the Indians dismounted they were completely out of sight.

Those Indians who had been unmounted were running hard to rejoin their more fortunate companions. It was slaughter, but there was nothing else for it – the party behind the rocks turned their guns on them and picked them off, one by one, so that in the end no more than two or three reached safety unhurt.

Then Redpath saw something feebly moving far away through the long grass. He watched for a while, then lifted his rifle and took deliberate aim.

For it was the renegade, Riarn, out there in the grass. Only Riarn was without scalp, to add to all the other horrors that had befallen him. The horse he and his escorting brave were riding must have been shot down in the mêlée. The Dog Man's immediate reaction must have been to scalp the tormented prisoner before attempting to escape himself – an action typical of the savage Dog Warriors.

Redpath squeezed his trigger. Riarn collapsed and lay still. The hunter had sent him where pain could never touch him again. . . .

Another, smaller party of Dog Men unexpectedly tried to race through to the buildings. Redpath and his followers' guns opened fire and toppled three or four Indians before the others sent their horses jumping for safety into the water of the tributary. The range was now rather great, but Redpath felt that even if the Dog Men rode close up to the water's edge his party would be able to stop most of the Indians from getting through.

What worried him most was the thought that any moment Indians from along the Powder River trails north and south of the settlement might come flooding out and catch his party in the rear. And he thought it was inevitable – within a short space of time it must happen.

He was no pessimist, but it seemed that there was to be no retreat from this situation – neither retreat nor escape. He kept seeing the picture of brown-haired, smiling-eyed Judith, the girl he had just won; but he tried to keep his thoughts from her, because it seemed that he would never see her again. All he hoped was that the settlers would be able to hold out against the Indians until Colonel Endricks sent aid to them from Fort Phil Kearney. He could do his bit by keeping these Indians from that ammunition cache as long as possible.

He saw feathered plumes bobbing along the bank of the tributary. The braves were showing sense. No longer were they trying to race through to their target; now they preferred to crawl along to it. It took longer, but it was a whole lot safer.

But the mere fact that they still persisted in heading for those worthless, tumbledown buildings suggested one important thing – they knew, at any rate, where to look for the ammunition among those buildings. It was a logical deduction, and Redpath felt he was safe in assuming that the secret had not died with the renegade.

It was galling to sit up in that vantage-point overlooking the farm and not be able to do anything to stop the cautious advance of the Dog Men towards their target. Once he saw a head, incautiously high, and snapped off a quick round, but it probably had no other result than to keep the Indian crawling a little lower after that.

Within minutes, Redpath guessed that already the first of the Indians must be very near the flimsy farm buildings. He sighed. 'Reckon there ain't much we c'n do now,' he heard someone mutter near to him, and he was forced to agree with the man.

Back of them now the fire from the village seemed to be a constant barrage of angry sound, while the smoke from dozens of burning buildings hung like a pall over the fast-flowing Powder River.

The man started to speak again, to say something else, but Redpath grabbed the man's arm and exclaimed, 'Quiet!'

At that they all listened – and heard.

Horsemen were approaching at a fast gallop from along the trail to their right – from the direction of the besieged commissioner's wagon. Their instant thought was, 'Reinforcements!' But not reinforcements for themselves – for the Indians down along the edge of the tributary!

The Dog Men down the gully must have thought so, too, for a few of them showed signs of mounting and riding out. Redpath ordered two of the men to keep watch on the gully, while he and the other three kept their rifles trained on the brow behind them.

Suddenly a mass of riders came flooding over the bare shoulder of the hill where the trail ran. Blue-coated riders – cavalrymen!

Then a swaying, lurching, covered wagon came thundering into view, and at that Redpath understood. For some reason the lieutenant must have broken through his circle of besiegers and was heading almost directly for them.

He stood up and shouted, because the way the party was riding they would end up among the Indians all along that tributary by the 'breeds' farm. He gesticulated in an effort to stop them, and the leading troopers must have recognized him, for they pulled off the trail and came heading for their rocky shelter. Promptly the Indians down the gully opened up with their three or four muzzle-loaders and lead came screaming up at them.

The lieutenant wasn't with this party. Redpath shouted to a sergeant in the lead, 'There's no way out down there. About forty Injuns hold the bank of that stream. Better hold up here with us.'

The sergeant got the meaning of his shouted words and gave an order to his men. At once they all came riding up among the boulders, the covered wagon almost toppling over as the lead horses turned at a sharp angle to follow the cavalry.

Then the rearguard came racing over the brow – the lieutenant and a dozen men holding back the Indians who had besieged them. As the officer came galloping up to the wagon, now standing among the big boulders, he shouted, 'Why did you come here?' Then he saw Redpath.

Everywhere men were dismounting and getting behind cover. Redpath reckoned that about forty had survived the fighting, though probably over half were wounded somewhere or other. He thought they were lucky to have got through with such comparative light losses.

The sergeant was explaining about the Indians who held the position ahead of them. The young officer looked annoyed.

'When we heard that firing so close we thought we must be almost on top of the settlement, so we broke out. Now we're in as bad a position as ever.'

Redpath said, tartly, 'I never asked you to come.' Then he saw Ann Churl standing up on the tailboard of the wagon. Behind her was her father.

CHAPTER FOURTEEN

AND IN THE END

Plainly the girl was terrified out of her wits – this Indian attack clearly had unnerved her. And her father's usually red face was white and drawn now.

Redpath called, 'You still got your old ideas about makin' friends with Injuns – by givin' 'em rifles, commissioner?' He couldn't forget that men were dying all around him, and more would still have to die because of this fat fool from the Indian Bureau in Washington.

Henry Churl just stood and said nothing. He had courage, as a lot of city men unexpectedly have, yet not sufficient to be able to admit his mistakes even at a time like that.

The pursuing Indians were blasted back off the skyline when they came riding over. In fact, the position the party occupied was a good defensive situation, even though in the end they were bound to be surrounded and cut off – and in the end wiped out. But all those white men there knew they would take heavy toll of the attacking Indians before that happened.

For about ten minutes they were subjected to sudden attacks from mounted Indians from the party that had ridden in after the cavalry, but all were driven off with heavy losses to the Dog Men, though they sustained some injuries themselves. In this second party more Indians had rifles, and some of them were Henrys, stripped from the bodies of the fallen cavalrymen who had died in the earlier fighting.

Hearing the bullets scream disconcertingly close into their midst, Redpath could imagine what it would be like if these fine marksmen secured ammunition for the five hundred Henry breech loaders they now possessed.

He turned his attention to those farm buildings below. By now there must be several Indians either among the buildings or very close to them. Within minutes, perhaps, they would have ammunition for the useless rifles that doubtless were strapped to every brave's horse.

The hunter watched that farm, as if by staring he could prevent it from being occupied by their enemies. And all the time he racked his brain, saying over and over again, 'There must be some way of stopping them – even now.'

But he couldn't think of any.

Then he saw a Dog Man come crawling over the lip of the gully, intent upon retrieving some muzzle-loader that lay out in the open. Redpath sighted carefully, fired and saw the brave roll over, kicking until he died.

But he saw something else. Just beyond the muzzle of Redpath's rifle a few stalks of dry grass took flame from the explosion, and as the white smoke drifted away he saw the flame leap to other grass nearby then die.

It gave him an idea. He sat and looked at those flimsy wooden buildings down on the bank of the stream. They would burn like tinder. The thought in his mind was, 'If you set fire to a building, you just can't get inside it.'

He determined to set fire to the 'breeds' farmhouse and adjoining buildings. The only problem was – how to do it?

And that was a problem. There was little cover all the way into the farm, and he knew he could never make it alive, especially now that the Indians were occupying the place. He decided if he couldn't take the fire to those buildings, then something else must do it.

The plan was in his mind in an instant, and he crawled across to where the youthful lieutenant was directing the defence. The boy – Redpath couldn't think of him as

146

anything else – had had part of his ear shot away, and a very red bandage now covered his fair, curly head, but he seemed entirely unruffled by his nearness to a more mortal injury and was apparently in his normal cheerful mood.

Redpath sat and talked to him. The lieutenant took time off to listen, then said, 'I think the plan's worth trying, Redpath. If it succeeds I propose to fight our way back into the settlement without further ado. We can mount the civilians up behind us.'

So they crawled across to the wagon. The commissioner and the two ladies were sitting underneath it, the picture of misery. Yet even then Redpath felt that the meek and timid Mrs Churl seemed far less affected than her husband or daughter. He wondered if she had suffered so much at the hands of the well-meaning but blundering commissioner that she no longer got excited over distressing circumstances.

Even now the hostility of the Indian commissioner towards Redpath was high and virulent. His daughter was the apple of his eye, and anyone who hurt her in his eyes committed an unforgivable sin. So Redpath was beyond forgiveness, of course.

Churl hardly listened to what the officer was saying. When he had finished he shouted. 'No, no, I will not permit it! I have articles of great value aboard that wagon, and I will not stand by and see them destroyed because of the whim of this man.'

The lieutenant said, patiently, 'It seems more than a whim to me, sir. I would call it plain necessity.'

The portly man, pale-faced with emotion, demanded, 'Why couldn't we have continued when we were on the move and made the settlement?'

'We didn't know where it was,' the officer remarked drily. 'We were heading for a nice little ambuscade when Redpath called us off.'

'But we could start off again. We know where the settlement is now. And there appear to be no Indians between us and the place.'

The young lieutenant's face became very cold. 'Sir,' he said very emphatically, 'we do not leave the place while there is a chance to help ourselves by destroying those buildings, which probably hide the ammunition down there.'

Regardless of the bullets that came zipping in among the rocks, Henry Churl struggled up to his feet. 'You were placed unreservedly at my orders.' His fat white face was trembling with passion. He was not the kind of man to allow his own inclinations to be overruled under any circumstances. And, anyway, it seemed that if they started off for the settlement now they stood a better chance of getting through safely than if after some prolonged experiments in pyrotechnics – of dubious value to them, anyway.

But that boy lieutenant settled things. He said curtly, 'I will take the consequences of disobeying your orders, sir. More, if you attempt to interfere with these plans, I shall order you to be shot down. This is no time for selfish obstinacy.'

'There,' thought the hunter admiringly, 'is a man – even if he is an irritatingly cocky young devil at times!'

Henry Churl's jaw sagged. It seemed impossible that such a threat could be directed against him. Perhaps in that moment he realized how far he had fallen from that proud position in Washington when he had been introduced as the Indian Office's special commissioner to the West. Now he was worse than a nonentity – he was despised and of such low account that there was this talk of shooting him out of hand to get rid of him!

His wife's tired voice came up to him. 'Sit down, Henry,' she ordered. 'Must you forever go on making's fool of yourself?' And she said in that moment what she had wanted to say in over thirty years of marriage, but which she had never before dared utter.

Now it pricked the conceit of that portly, arrogant man, her husband. He seemed to collapse. If his meek and timid wife could turn against him, then anything was possible. He looked stupidly at his white-faced, terrified daughter and the thought came again to his mind – 'Anything's possible.'

The commissioner and his family were led out of danger while Redpath and a trooper went within the covered wagon and prepared it for its most useful moment.

They turned out everything combustible and piled it in a great heap in the centre of the big prairie schooner – spare clothing, some of it of great price in those places where clothes were much cherished, blankets and straw bedding – especially the straw-filled mattresses. Then they emptied a five-gallon can of lamp oil over the pile, and turned out the contents of three lamps on to it besides.

That done the wagon was unhitched from its team of horses, which were allowed to trot away out of range of the firing; then the wagon was shoved out into the open, in a position directly above the farm buildings.

The limber was locked. Then Redpath said, 'That okay, lootenant?'

'I think so.'

'Think it'll go straight an' hit that big barn down there?'

The lieutenant said, calmly, 'If it doesn't we're doomed to stay here and fight on until they get that ammunition into their Henrys. Then I guess we won't stay fighting much longer.' Not with a couple of hundred braves against them, armed with the new breech-loading rifles.

There was nothing more they could do. Now they just had to trust that the wagon would keep on a straight course and set fire to the farm buildings when it crashed.

Redpath struck a match and lit some kerosene-soaked cloth. Some bullets were coming in among them from the Indians back up the brow, though a screen of rocks partly shielded them, so Redpath quickly slung the burning rag into the wagon and at once three or four troopers put their backs to it and set it rolling. Once it was on the move they all dived hurriedly back under cover.

Everybody watched with desperate anxiety as the wagon slowly gathered speed and went crashing down that long, sloping hillside. At first there was no sign of burning from within, and Redpath wondered if they had been precipitous in shoving off, but suddenly a great gout of flame came belching out from the rear as the draught under the cover fanned up a raging fire.

There was a cheer from the troopers at that, and further cheering as the flaming wagon careered at a mad pace straight down towards those buildings, two hundred yards or more away.

Then they groaned. The prairie schooner was seen to be running away from the buildings – it was now beginning to head just past them and would end up in the stream.

Almost when it seemed they had failed, the wagon must have run into a little rise which pulled the head round – and with a crash it caught the protruding end of the long, low barn and brought it staggering on top of the flaming canvas cover.

Actually it couldn't have been better for them; for the tumbling roof fell right into the blazing fire, and within minutes the whole building was a roaring mass of flame.

Redpath was content. The southerly wind that was steadily blowing would drive those flames across any gap until every building on that farm was ablaze.

A kid was jerking his elbow, shouting, 'I told you, didn't I? There's somebody down in that farm!'

Everybody stared. Men were staggering through the flames, their hands held over their faces as a protection against the intense heat. And these weren't Indians – these were dressed in white man's garb.

There were six or seven of them. Perhaps they had been hiding inside the very barn that had been fired by the runaway wagon. As they came staggering into the open their clothes were seen to be on fire, and not all the beating of their hands could put it out.

A cry of horror rose from every man up there on the knoll, for the desperate men, maddened by their burns, were running towards the cool waters of the tributary.

And the lusting, blood-savage Dog Men were there, waiting for them.

As they came almost within reach of the stream, an arrow

caught the first burning man and he went down. Then a hail of arrows came and dropped every man as he ran.

Redpath heard the shaken voice of Henry Churl. 'What a way to die! Who were those men? What were they doing there?'

The hunter said slowly, 'I'll guess one of 'em was a *hombre* you know – a treacherous 'breed called – Joe Loup. Maybe some of the others were whites. If so they'd be Stuart an' Jep Connor. The rest'd be Loup's 'breed relatives – them 'Injuns' that stuck you up that day, commissioner.'

The commissioner could only mutter, 'What a way to die!'

Redpath went across to his horse. He was trying to figure out how those men came to be there in those buildings. The 'breed girl had told him that they had ridden away at first notice that Indians were expected to attack the settlement. He wondered if they had run into a party of Indians – maybe some Cheyennes already on the west bank, riding up in response to that smoke signal from their relatives, the Dog Soldiers. If so they might have retreated back to their farm, not daring to show their faces within the settlement. That would explain those horses wandering loose about the place.

It was an appalling way to die, as the commissioner had said, but all the same Redpath wasn't inclined to waste much sympathy on the renegades just then.

He was watching some Indians, covered by the dense clouds of smoke, streaking across towards the farm buildings in an effort to salvage the ammunition before the flames got to it. Redpath couldn't move, even though everyone else was mounting in preparation for the breakout to the settlement. He had come here determined to prevent the Indians from getting away with that precious ammunition. He was in agony lest at the very last moment he should see his plans balked—

And then flames rose into the air, sparks went soaring for fully a hundred and fifty feet, and with them went burning spars of timber. A fraction of a second later a dull boom of an explosion came to their ears.

At that everyone cheered like mad. For no Indian can make use of ammunition which has been exploded by fire. That ammunition would no longer be a threat to the settlers, and now they could return within the defences knowing that their mission had been successfully accomplished.

Redpath leapt across for his horse. The portly commissioner was up behind the lightest trooper in the party; other troopers were hoisting the timid Mrs Henry Churl to a place where she could cling behind a sergeant. Now there was competition for the fair but frightened Ann.

Yet she refused all offers of aid from the soldiers. Instead she came running across to the hunter, just about to mount. She whispered in agony, 'I'm sorry – forgive me – it was so wrong what I did. I – I don't want to live, I am so ashamed!'

And a lot of people heard it, including the young lieutenant – and the portly commissioner, her fond father.

She was hysterical, beside herself with fear and mortification; and yet something inside her demanded that at this moment she should atone for all the wrong she had done to this man – perhaps she felt that now she was about to die, and she didn't want to go leaving a man to bear forever the shame that had come with her slandering tongue.

'I didn't know what I was saying. I must have been crazy—'

'Yeah, maybe you were,' said the hunter gently, bending. 'But we're all a little crazy at times.'

And then he stooped and took her in his arms and swung her on to his horse before him. Next moment the whole cavalcade went racing out the back way, determined to fight their way into the settlement.

It was surprisingly easy. There must have been some natural obstacle to the north of that knoll which delayed a circling movement by the Indians who had followed the lieutenant's party. Only a few had managed to get through, and these were all afoot, and only one had a rifle.

The horsemen and their burdens thundered down upon these hapless Indians. All in one moment the triumph that the Dog Soldiers were anticipating changed to a knowledge that death was to be their lot from this bold attack upon the white man's settlement.

Every Indian was cut down or shot, and only one trooper came off his horse. Even he came running in unharmed, minutes later.

A cheer floated out to them from the nearest defence posts. The sight of those blue uniforms – reinforcements for their tiny garrison – must have been very heartening. They pounded through the posts, racing for the store, that centre of operations for the besieged settlers. They found a lot of wounded there, having their injuries attended to by the womenfolk – and some dead, their shrouds rough blankets from Mike Grew's store. One – but the hunter didn't know it – was old Lem.

Mike Grew wasn't to be seen, but the bearded patriarch, the defence commander, was there, receiving reports and issuing orders.

And Judith was with them, attending to the wounded.

Everyone looked up as the cavalry came sweeping in between the buildings. The hunter saw Judith's eyes widen with astonishment as they fell on the girl before him.

But this was no time for explanations. He lowered Ann to the ground, shouted, 'Look after her, Judith – she needs it.' Then he went wheeling off towards the sound of nearby fighting.

Judith looked at the pale, frightened girl, her former mistress; then her big heart took pity on her. She came forward, put her arm round her and led her to a seat. Ann was crying quietly for a long time afterwards, but then Judith put bandages into her hands and though they trembled they found solace in tending to those less fortunate than herself.

There was savage fighting back among the defence posts to the south of the settlement. The attack from up-river had been unexpected, and the Indians had secured a footing within the defence positions before their onrush was halted. So it was that a string of huts was in fact isolated from the main body of settlers, though they were still putting up a fight against their enemies.

Redpath saw mounted Dog Soldiers, screaming their savage war whoops, riding in and out of the huts, charging at them and killing before being driven away. The Indians were in such numbers that, attacked as they were from all sides, those isolated defence posts must soon have succumbed to the never-ceasing onslaughts.

As he watched, the firing ended from within one stout-walled cabin. Triumphant Dog Soldiers rode in and battered down the door, then flung themselves inside. After a few seconds they came pouring out in a mob, and in their midst were a few desperately struggling settlers.

Redpath didn't watch to see their awful fate. He guessed that the post had fallen because the defenders had run out of ammunition. Probably those other isolated defence posts were in much the same condition. Something had to be done, because probably a quarter of their force was contained in those few cabins.

He went back to where the youthful lieutenant was talking tactics with the settlers' leader. He interrupted: 'There's a job for you an' your men right now, lootenant,' and he explained the desperate condition of those isolated defenders. 'Reckon your troop of cavalry could clear out the Injuns from among them huts an' then we'd have a better chance of standin' siege until Colonel Endricks sends relief.'

The lieutenant's answer was a shout to his men to fall in behind him. As they thundered out towards the battle-ground the hunter heard the lieutenant call, 'I hope to come out of this alive, Redpath – if only for your sake. If I do you won't have to worry about that charge against you. I heard the girl.'

The hunter shouted back, 'That's a relief!' He made it sound a joke, but he was thinking what this meant to Judith and himself. He could go anywhere now with the girl, settle and live without fear. His thoughts returned to those cattle lands he had seen down Palo Duro in Texas. That was the place for him.

Then they were racing across to where triumphant warriors were setting fire to the captured cabin. The sudden, savage onrush of troopers caught them unawares. A volley fired on the run put half the Indians out of the fight immediately, and then it came to cut and thrust and wild, sweeping blows with the butt end of their rifles.

Redpath saw a painted face and shot it, then he emptied his Sharps into a group who were coming towards them to break the charge – and then he was right in among them, his Colt flaming. His horse charged into a chief's pony and they all went down in a heap. Above them hoofs stabbed, Indian lances flashed, guns swung and the lieutenant's sword rose and fell.

He rolled, and the chief came over, tomahawk swinging. They fought, with a battle raging above their heads. Then Redpath got hold of the tomahawk arm and forced it back and kept on forcing until something broke. He hit the Indian with his own tomahawk and then staggered to his feet and went into battle with the Dog Chief's weapon cutting and hacking—

And then, surprisingly, unexpectedly, their little battle was all over. Suddenly the cavalry was in complete possession of the ground behind the defence posts.

The presence of the army men put new hope and enthusiasm into the hearts of the defenders. The bearded old man was walking from post to post shouting, 'Now we c'n hold out agen them varmints! Don't let 'em get through your line. Hold out until tomorrow mornin' an' we'll have a relief column a-comin' in.'

The battle for Sweet Water was won and lost with that cavalry charge, which threw out the red attackers from behind the defence posts. The fighting wasn't over by any means – time after time the Indians came storming in even through the defence positions, but always they were shot down or sent flying back.

The attack diminished with darkness. Probably the chiefs were arguing by now, 'Our plans have gone astray. We only attacked this paleface settlement for the ammunition we were told we would obtain there. But that is gone. Why, then, lose more men in attacking this settlement? What good will it bring us if we do capture it?'

It took some time to pull the bloodthirsty Dog Soldiers out of the attack, but in the end it was done. Then, with the shades of evening, the firing slowly petered out and there was silence.

Big fires were lit in the open space by Mike Grew's store, to keep warm all those who could not find shelter within the few remaining cabins. When his turn on duty ended at one of the posts, Redpath walked in beside his tired mount, worn out and weary, wanting only sleep now.

Judith was waiting for him. She had blankets and she spread them close to a fire. She made him lie down; she knew how exhausted he must be after the last thirty-six hours' activity. But she sat close to him while he closed his eyes and prepared for sleep. He spoke to her, at first lucidly, then as sleep thickened his tongue, slowly and less coherently.

Judith bent over him. 'Sleep, dear, don't talk. We'll have a lot of time for talk in the years when we are married.'

'Married?' His lips twitched into a smile. 'I can't believe it, honey. Just hold my hand, will you? I want to make sure this ain't no dream. Let me hold it – I don't ever want to let go of it—'

And when the cavalry from Fort Phil Kearney came trotting down the trail before first light that morning, unexpectedly early, Judith was still sitting beside the sleeping hunter holding his hand – holding it because she couldn't get her hand free without disturbing him.

When Jim Redpath, army scout and hunter, got his hands on to anything good he wasn't the kind to let go. And he reckoned in Judith he had got something good – the best thing he'd had in all his adventurous life.

156